KEEP LAUGHING

BOOKS BY CYNTHIA D. GRANT

Kumquat May, I'll Always Love You
Phoenix Rising: Or How to Survive Your Life
Keep Laughing

KEEP
LAUGHING

Cynthia D. Grant

ATHENEUM • *1991* • *NEW YORK*

Maxwell Macmillan Canada
TORONTO

Maxwell Macmillan International
NEW YORK OXFORD SINGAPORE SYDNEY

Atheneum
Macmillan Publishing Company
866 Third Avenue
New York, NY 10022

Maxwell Macmillan Canada, Inc.
1200 Eglinton Avenue East
Suite 200
Don Mills, Ontario M3C 3N1

Macmillan Publishing Company is part of the Maxwell Communication Group of Companies.

First edition

Printed in the United States of America

10 9 8 7 6 5 4 3 2 1

The text of this book is set in 12/16 Korinna

LIBRARY OF CONGRESS CATALOGING-IN-PUBLICATION DATA

Grant, Cynthia D.
    Keep laughing / Cynthia D. Grant.
    p.   cm.
    Summary: A famous comedian attempts a reunion with the teenage son he abandoned years ago.
    ISBN 0–689–31514–7
    [1. Fathers and sons—Fiction.   2. Comedians—Fiction.]
I. Title.
PZ7.G76672Ke   1991
[Fic]—dc20   91-6816

Book design by Eliza Green

For
Gretchen, Genevieve, and Kathy B.,
three of the best

Hello, everybody! It's great to be here! Gee, you're a terrific-looking audience! And I want you to know I really mean that, from the bottom of my wallet.

No, but seriously, I know what you're thinking: What's a fifteen-year-old kid know about comedy?

My childhood was a joke! A laugh riot! A continual yuk fest! My childhood—yukkk!

Sir, you could do better? Want to tone down the heckling?

What? Why it's Dad! I should've known.

Just kidding. My father's not really here. He's lost in television land. He's a professional funnyman. Joey Young. You've probably seen him on the tube. That's where I usually see him. In fact, until I was ten years old, I thought he was six inches tall!

You know how kids are. We get confused. I used

to think he worked for the post office. Whenever he showed up, he was delivering packages! Here's a Tonka truck; that's for missing your birthday. Here's an Etch-A-Sketch; that's for missing last year.

He'd look around my mother's house and say: "You're living in squalor!" I thought squalor was the name of our town!

My folks were divorced when I was a baby, so I hardly know Joey. He breezes in and out. When I was a little boy he taught me a rhyme. He said: "Roses are red, violets are blue, I'll stick to you like gum on your shoe. That's how I feel about you, Sport." Then he disappeared for six months!

But hey, I'm not complaining. What's the point? You can gripe all you want; it won't change a thing. Joey was busy, he was pushing his career. He'd get in a bad mood when he was working on his act. His face would be all frazzled and frowning. You'd think he was worried about world peace or something. Then suddenly he'd shout: "See, this dog goes into a bar..." But hey, it's tough to be funny. This is some crazy world. I mean, you can get shot or stabbed or strangled, or trampled to death at a garage sale. They keep asking me at school: What do you want to be when you grow up?

I say: Alive.

God bless you, you're a wonderful group! Joey always brings out God to take a bow, in case he's been sounding like a wise guy. Does he really believe in God? You're asking the wrong guy. I'm only his son; I don't know him personally!

People think comedians are naturally funny. Not true! A comedian is the saddest guy around! It's like hiring a pyromaniac to be the fire chief! Sure, he's an expert in his field, but is he the right man for the job?

Thank you so much! I want to leave you with a thought: He who laughs, lasts, and he who cries, dies. So no matter what happens, keep laughing! Don't stop!

No matter what happens, keep laughing.

KEEP LAUGHING

CHAPTER ONE

My mother and I were watching my father on television. It was the first time we'd seen him in almost two years.

"He looks pretty good," she said. "Joey never changes."

"Neither do his jokes." He was doing the bit about how he suffers from Mickey Rooney syndrome. No matter how old he gets, he says, he still looks like a baby.

Ma said, "He's coming to see you."

"When?"

"Tomorrow night, for dinner."

"You're kidding."

"Would I kid about something like that?" she said. There is nothing more serious than a comedian's ex-wife. Except a comedian. "You be here."

"I have basketball practice."

"In the summertime? I mean it, Shepherd. Do you read me?"

Sorry, you're not coming in, I radioed into the transmitter built into my flight suit. Your signal is breaking up. Over and out... Just ahead, beyond the bubble of my star-streaked windshield, virgin galaxies unfolded. Court-martial or not, I would keep going, even if it meant fighting every alien in the universe—

"Shepherd, are you listening?"

"Of course I'm listening." I played back what she'd said, word for word. Part of my brain had inhaled it like a tape recorder, while another part sailed on and on... Sometimes I'm somewhere else so completely, that when I come back, it's a shock. Then I'll say, "Yes, Ma" or "A dependent clause contains a subject and a verb," depending on where I am, and that gets me off the hook.

"Why's he coming tomorrow night?" I asked. "Is it Christmas or my birthday?" Not that those dates are special. Joey forgot all about them last year.

"He wants to see you."

"Send him a picture."

Joey hasn't called me in months. I can't call him because I never know where he is. My friends say, I saw your father on TV. Lately he's been on cable a lot but we can't afford a hookup.

My mother said, "Be nice, Shepherd. Don't hurt his feelings."

Sometimes she talks about him like he's a child. For a while he used the line "Be nice!" in his act. "Be nice!" he'd warn the audience when they groaned at his jokes. He was hoping it'd catch on and become his trademark.

On the tube Joey launched into some ex-wife stuff. The woman he describes is total fiction, not Ma.

"He has a surprise for you," Ma said. She was curled up on the couch, munching popcorn. Like Joey, she's small. I'm six feet tall. Meet my parents, Mr. and Mrs. Tiny Tim. "He's going to call you right after the show," she added.

He didn't. Finally I went to bed. Three hours later my mother woke me up. "Joey wants to talk to you," she said.

I took the call on the phone in the kitchen. The first thing he said was, "How'd you like the show?" Not, "Gee, I'm sorry I woke you up," or "How are you?" or any niceties like that.

"Fine."

"It went over real good. They loved me."

"Yeah."

"What's the matter with you? How come you sound so grumpy?"

"Dad, I was asleep."

3

"You sound like a zombie. The least you could do is say congratulations."

"I thought you were going to call right after the show."

"I couldn't get to a phone," he said. "What time is it, anyway?"

"Late."

"Well, listen, I've got terrific news. I'm moving to San Francisco! I'll only be an hour away! Shep, are you there? Did you hear me?"

"Yeah."

"Aren't you glad?"

"Dad—"

"I thought you'd be pleased!"

"I am! I'm asleep! Will you give me a break?"

"Well, remind me never to call you if I win a million dollars. I don't want to interrupt your beauty sleep."

"When will I see you?"

"I'm flying up tomorrow. I'm so sick of L.A. So you liked the act?"

"Sure."

"It went over great. You should've seen the studio audience. They went crazy! Did you catch me on the 'Midnight Rambler' show?"

"No," I said. "We don't get cable."

"How's school?"

"It's summer vacation now."

4

"Duh, yeah. I mean last year. Eighth grade."

"I was in ninth grade last year."

"You're kidding. Geez, time sure flies. I've got a high school reunion coming up. Twenty years since I escaped, can you believe it? Well, hey, get some rest. I'll see you tomorrow night. And Sport, tell your mother not to make that stuff she always makes. The Jell-O with the hair."

"Those are alfalfa sprouts," I said, but Joey had already hung up.

CHAPTER TWO

Swampy was on the phone. He said, "Can you come over? My folks are fighting bad."

"What do you want me to do? Break it up?" I asked.

"Just hang out. We could watch a movie. They act a lot nicer when people are here."

"I can't," I said. "My father's coming over tonight and I have to help my mom get ready."

"Did you see him on TV last night? He was funny. It must be neat having a star for your dad."

"Yeah, right," I said. Swampy gets cable. He sees Joey more often than I do.

"Want to shoot some baskets at Kleiser later? I'll pick you up."

"I'll have to check with my mom. I'll call you back," I said.

My mother was doing what she does every Saturday morning: cleaning, cleaning, cleaning. She cleans things that aren't even dirty. "I like the place to look nice," she says. Which isn't easy; the house is so old and crummy it's falling apart while she's sweeping.

Sometimes I feel sorry for my mother. I'd like to buy her things. She wears the same old clothes so she can get me stuff. She doesn't make a lot of money at her job and my father probably can't send her much. He doesn't work steadily.

"Swampy wants to know if I can go to Kleiser Park later."

"Is his mother going?"

"To shoot hoops? I doubt it."

"Why can't you play at City Park?" Ma asked.

We've been over this a million times. "Because the baskets are only six feet high."

"Well, does Swampy have to drive? Can't you walk or ride your bikes?"

"Yeah, but we wouldn't get there till tomorrow. It's ten miles."

My mother shook her head. "I don't think so, Shepherd."

"Ma, will you please—"

"Aren't you supposed to be mowing the lawn?"

"I mean when I'm done."

"We'll talk about it then." My mother swept into the bathroom and began to scrub the sink.

Lately we've been having problems. We used to

get along fine. Around the time I turned thirteen she really changed. Hormones or midlife crisis, or something. She gets mad or weepy all the time, over nothing.

It's weird to be able to look down at the top of her head. She used to seem so big. I kid her, I tell her she's shrinking. She says, "I feel like it."

She still won't let me take driver's training. When I bring it up, she changes the subject. I'll be sixteen in November. She won't let me grow up. She doesn't want me to drive or even ride with my friends. She says, "You're my baby. You're all I've got."

I say, "Ma, I'm not a baby."

"I know you're not," she says. "But to me you'll always be my baby."

She likes to look at my pictures in the photograph albums. "See how cute you were!" she says, showing me a fat kid who always looks like he just lost a food fight. The other day she told Swampy she used to call me Pudding Pants. "Really!" he said. I knew I'd hear about that later.

I can picture the scene at my high school graduation.

The principal says, "It is a great honor to present this year's valedictorian, Shepherd "Pudding Pants" Youngman. Shep, will you step forward, please?"

The audience goes wild. They're screaming and applauding.

8

"We have a big surprise for you, Shepherd," the principal says. Not only have you received a full scholarship to Harvard, based on your 6.0 grade point average, your basketball scores, and your incredible good looks, but I have also been authorized to offer you the presidency of Harvard University. You can earn while you learn. What do you say, Pudding Pants?"

The crowd holds its breath.

"I don't know," I say. "I'll have to ask my mom. Can I, Ma? Please?"

I'm not looking forward to seeing my father. It's always kind of strange. He rushes in and hugs me and acts like he wants me to sit on his lap, but who the hell is he? I don't even know him. He moved out when I was a baby. There are pictures of him and me in the albums. Joey's usually holding me like I'm a Ming vase. A Ming vase full of dirty diapers.

He has not been a major factor in my life. We hear more from our insurance guy than we do from Joey.

My mother finished policing the bathroom and looked out the window at the front lawn. I was sitting on the couch reading a newspaper.

She said, "I thought I told you to do the lawn."

"I did."

"With what? Your teeth?"

"It looks fine to me."

"You missed a spot," she said. "Like half of it."

9

"It's that crummy mower. We need an electric mower."

"For a lawn that size? You could do it with manicure scissors. Why do you have to be so lazy?"

"I'm not lazy! That mower's no good!"

My mother said, "Why don't you buy the kind you can ride around on, so you can read the newspaper while you're doing it?"

"Why bother? You wouldn't let me drive it."

"Not with that attitude."

"What attitude?" I said. "You're the one who started it! That lawn mower is a million years old!"

"So buy a new one!"

"Right. I'm Mr. Moneybags. Sure."

I baby-sit and do odd jobs. I could get a real job at Gartini's Market, delivering groceries to senior citizens. Mrs. G. said she'll hire me when I get my license. Unless she hires someone else first. Since her son left for college, she's been making all the deliveries and ends up missing her soap opera. I could make some money and get a few tips, and I could drive around in the store's station wagon. It's old but it's got a great tape deck.

"Listen to me, Shepherd," my mother said, "when I ask you to do something, do it. Don't make excuses. You say you want to be treated like an adult, but you act like a baby."

"I'm not acting like a baby!"

"This isn't a dude ranch and you are not the head dude. I work all day—" She's a secretary for the school district. She hates it. "You are not the Little Prince. Are you listening to me, Shepherd?"

"I am not the Little Prince. It's a matter of perspective. The lawn looks fine to me."

"But you're going to fix it. Am I making myself clear?"

Her eyes were a foot lower than mine. If I walked out on her, she couldn't stop me. But I could never walk out on Ma. Lightning would strike me. The sky would explode. It would be the end of civilization as we know it, at least at our house.

"Don't get in a sweat," I said. "I'll take care of it."

This always happens when my father comes to visit. Ma and I get real tense, we fight. It's easier to deal with him on the phone. It's easier for Joey too. Four or five years ago we saw him more often. Since then he's been in New York, Los Angeles, Las Vegas, even Europe, keeping his career going. It's always like his big break is just around the corner. He never quite makes it, but he never flunks out. He's the opening act for a lot of top comedians.

Joey's had parts in a couple of movies too. One did okay, one bombed. He recorded an album, *You Were Expecting Someone Else?* I guess they were, because the album died. That line was Joey's trademark for a while. There's an old movie called *Mighty*

11

Joe Young, about a giant ape who played second banana to King Kong. When Joey did talk shows, he'd have himself introduced as Mighty Joey Young, then he'd run onstage and when the applause died down, he'd say, "You were expecting someone else?" Nobody got it. The movie was too old, Joey said, too dated. He's as desperate to find a signature line as scientists are to cure cancer.

My friends think he's a big success. None of their fathers are on TV, but they're around, even the divorced ones. You don't have to turn on the tube to see them. When Joey comes to visit it's like we've just been introduced and we have to get used to each other again. Appearing live, for one night only, tonight's special guest—your father!

I've waited for him. I've waited for phone calls and letters and birthday cards that didn't come. He promised we'd do so many things together: go to the zoo, to the beach, hear music. We never did.

When he'd leave me, he'd say, "See you later, Alligator!"

"In a while, Crocodile!" I'd say. I thought he made that up. I thought he was the smartest guy in the world. I thought he was a lot of things he wasn't.

How can you have a kid and not care about him; not even wonder how he is or what he's doing? Like he's nothing, not even your flesh and blood.

I guess I was expecting someone else too.

12

CHAPTER THREE

My father slipped into town like the Rose Bowl Parade, tooting his horn all the way down the block. He likes an audience. By the time he parked his '63 Galaxie in our driveway, kids were jumping up and down in the yard, while their fathers, washing and waxing their own cars, watched from across the street.

"That's not a car, it's a yacht," my mother said, looking out the living room window. "Geez, what a lousy time to quit smoking." She stuffed a Baby Ruth into her mouth. Since she quit, a month ago, she's hit the junk food, hard.

I went outside. The car was a baby blue convertible. Classic. My father was just putting up the top.

"Shep, can you give me a hand?" he called.

So I applauded him.

One of the kids pointed at Joey and shouted,

"You're funny! You're on TV!" Another kid asked him for his autograph.

"Sure," Joey said, "as long as it's not on a check." He scribbled his name on a scrap of paper.

"Come here, Sport," he said and threw an arm around my shoulder. "Either you're taking steroids or I'm standing in a ditch. I *am* standing in a ditch! Who's been shelling the driveway? Is your mother trying to trap a rhino or what?"

We went into the house. My mother and father hugged very briefly, the way you frisk somebody to see if they're carrying weapons. Joey took off his jacket and tossed it on the couch. He was dressed in black, with a gold chain at his throat. His eyes looked tired but his face looked young.

"Carolyn, do you mind if I park the car in here? I'm afraid it'll get stripped if I leave it outside. I hate to tell you this but the neighborhood's gone downhill. You should sell the place and move."

"Good idea," Ma said. "Unfortunately, we don't own the house."

"Oh, yeah," Joey said. "Do you mind if I smoke?" The ash on his cigarette was an inch long.

"I'll get you an ashtray," Ma said. "Sit down."

"Not in that chair," I said. "There's a spring coming out."

My mother escaped into the kitchen where she proceeded to make an ashtray, I guess. It seemed like

14

she was gone for a month. My father tapped his ashes into a potted plant. We looked at each other.

"So, Sport!" he announced. "It's good to see you. It's been a while."

"Almost two years," I said.

"No." Joey shook his head. "That's impossible."

I shrugged. There was no sense in arguing. Joey's my father and he's not my father. He's like the shine on something. He's not the something.

"What's with the hair?" he asked referring to my braid. It's very long and very thin and gets tucked down my shirt for school pictures. "From the front you look like the all-American boy; from behind you look like the all-American faggot."

"Words of wisdom from the all-American redneck."

"Hey! Don't talk to your father like that."

"It's okay for you to say whatever you want and I'm supposed to sit here and take it?"

"The point is, you're a good-looking kid. Why do you want to screw it up?"

"I'm not screwing it up."

My mother reappeared, bearing a tray of cheese and crackers.

"Oh, Joey, I forgot your ashtray," she said and disappeared.

"That's okay, while you were gone I quit smoking," he said, then lit another cigarette. Ma put the ashtray on the coffee table.

"Dinner should be ready in a little while," she said. "Joey, would you like a glass of wine?"

"Chardonnay, if you've got it," he said.

She looked blank. "I have white or red."

"In the fifty-gallon drums? Never mind, I'll take a beer if you've got one."

We sipped and munched and had the kind of sparkling conversation that the mannequins have when Sears closes for the night.

"So, Carolyn, how's your job?"

"Terrible. I hate it. I've gone back to school."

She takes a night class at the junior college. She wants to be a family counselor, like the woman she's been seeing, who's helping her to figure out her life.

"So, Shep," Joey said. "How's school?"

Et cetera. Dinner was finally ready. Joey talked about himself for a while; then the conversational well went bone dry. My father kept sneaking peeks at his watch like he had to catch a train and was hoping it would come through the dining room.

It's hard to imagine that my parents were married. They don't match; they're not alike. Joey left home when he was sixteen (so he says) and married my mother when he was twenty. He told her he was twenty-five. He told her he'd traveled extensively in Europe and had graduated from Oxford University. He told her all kinds of stuff and she believed him.

My mother couldn't tell a lie if you held a gun to her head. Joey does it for a living.

He's told so many lies about himself I think he gets confused. He remembers how he felt and believes that's the truth. Like he says: "My dad never loved me." Grampa's always loved him, but he's not the kind of person who could put that into words. Joey lies about his age. Last year in *TV Guide* he said he was thirty-two. I think he's thirty-eight. The article made it sound like he grew up poor. He didn't. His real name is Joseph Youngman, which he never mentions for publication. He told me he changed it because he was afraid he'd be confused with Henny Youngman, and because his new name sounds so up and bubbly. In his act he says he had a mixed marriage; he was married and his wife was mixed-up. Joey's family is Jewish, but my mother's not, so we celebrate everything. Ma's big on celebrating.

Joey's routines make it sound like he's just telling you the truth about his life, but none of it really happened, or he's got it all turned around. Joey wasn't the poor guy being screamed at by the crazy waiter; he was the crazy guy screaming at the poor waiter, in real life.

When he tells me stuff, it's hard to know whether it actually happened, if it might happen, or if he wants it to happen so badly he's convinced himself it did happen and has forgotten that he made it up. Comedians should be listed in medical dictionaries next to people who think Elvis is alive and well and running a bowling alley in Mississippi.

"How come you let Shep wear his hair like that?" my father asked, pretending to be joking.

"It's his head," my mother said.

"But he doesn't have to look at it."

"Neither do you," I said. "You're never here."

"Who am I, the Invisible Man?"

"Usually," I said.

"Shepherd," Ma said, "don't be rude."

I'm surprised she's let me keep my braid. She's usually real uptight. That's one reason she's going to the counselor; to figure out how to let go of me a little. She says, "I've taken care of you all your life. How am I supposed to stop?"

My father said, "I'm telling you, it looks ridiculous. You're a handsome kid. Cut it off."

This is how it is when my father comes to visit. He hasn't seen me in ages, but he's full of helpful hints. It would be like a stranger walking up to someone on the street and saying, "Take my advice, get a nose job."

The phone rang. I was praying it was for me so I could leave the table, but it was Jack, this guy Ma's been seeing. She met him in class. One time he said he'd come out and shoot some hoops with me but they got talking and he forgot. He makes her laugh a lot. I don't know why; he's not that funny.

My father glanced at his watch for the hundredth time. He said, "I've got to get back to the club."

His big news tonight was that he's part owner of a new comedy club in San Francisco. He says it's a great career opportunity that he couldn't pass up. He gets to be the host and also try out new material.

While he told us all this I tried to figure out if this was a step up the ladder, or down. Joey makes everything about his career sound great. He wants to be big. I mean huge. I mean Mighty Joey Young, with movies and albums and concert dates, and his own prime time TV show. What will happen to Joey if it doesn't work out?

"Sport, I want you to come see my new apartment," he said. "It's only an hour from here, right in the city."

"Sure," I said.

"Great. Soon as it's all fixed up." Joey looked at his watch again. A Rolex. Real or fake? He ducked into the kitchen and waved at my mother, who was still on the phone, yukking it up. She covered the mouthpiece and said, "Bye, Joey. Take care."

I followed him outside to his car.

"Like it?" he said. "I'll let you drive it sometime."

"I don't have a license yet."

"Why not?"

"I'm only fifteen. I've taken driver's ed, but Ma won't let me take driver's training."

"What's the problem?"

I shrugged. "She's afraid I'll get killed or something."

"I'll talk to her." Joey lit a cigarette. "Hey, I just thought of something. I've got that reunion coming up. The whole family's invited. You want to go?"

"When is it?"

"Couple of weeks. It's no big deal. I just thought you'd get a kick out of it. I might rent a limo."

"What's wrong with this car?"

"Nothing, obviously. I'd just do it as a kind of joke," he said. "The big star, you know."

"You could rent a family too. The wife, the kids, the dog—"

Joey reached behind me and tugged my braid. "See ya, Pocahontas. I'll be in touch."

I went back into the house. My mother was doing the dishes. "It's always so strange to see him," she said.

"Why did you marry him?"

"Why do you think? I loved him."

"How? The guy is such a jerk! He only cares about himself."

"Oh, Joey's not so bad," she said. "I feel sorry for him."

"Sorry for him! He's driving around in a classic car and you're sitting here in a slum, with nothing."

My mother smiled. "I've got you," she said.

20

CHAPTER FOUR

I'm sorry, sweetie," Mrs. Gartini said, "but I had to hire someone else."

I sagged against the meat counter, clutching my chest. "You're kidding. Tell me you're kidding," I said.

"I was tired of making the deliveries," she said. "They were interfering with my soap."

This insane TV show she watches every afternoon. She calls it "The Haunted Village."

"You've broken my heart," I said. "You've crushed my spirit."

"I knew I could count on you to take it like a man," she said. "Help yourself to a Pepsi."

She was sitting on a tall stool behind the counter, next to her husband, who was cutting up meat. I've known the Gartinis all my life. Their little store is on the corner of two busy streets, in the shadow of a high-rise retirement center.

I turned up the pressure. "You promised me a job."

"You can have a job, Shepherd. You can stock the shelves."

"You've dashed my hopes and dreams on the rocks of reality."

"Speaking of reality," Mrs. Gartini said, "it's time for 'The Haunted Village.'" She turned on the TV set perched behind the counter. Mr. Gartini gave me a sympathetic smile as he sliced up a chicken.

"Who did you hire?" I asked over the rising tide of theme music.

"One of your friends, I think. Sheila Richardson. She'll be here in a little while."

The final nail in my coffin. Sheila the She-Monster. I handed a carving knife to Mrs. Gartini.

"Here," I said. "You can finish the job. Then you can slice me up and sell me in sandwiches. Hey, speaking of luncheon meat, one of the reefers is leaking. You better put a lifeguard on that puddle, I'm not kidding."

Mrs. Gartini looked pained and patient. She said, "Sheila has her license, Shepherd. Plain and simple."

"And you'd rather give the job to somebody you hardly know, rather than wait a few months—okay, years, maybe—until you can give it to a kid who's practically like your own son."

"Shepherd," Mrs. Gartini sighed. "You're drowning

out Lawrence and Melanie. Today they're bound to find out that Roger's really a Nazi. They've been dragging it out for weeks."

I've watched several episodes of "The Haunted Village." People's problems never get solved; they just get worse. Right around the time somebody's coming out of a coma, they get framed for murder, or their kid gets amnesia, or their psychiatrist turns out to be psychotic. You'd think they'd notice there's a voodoo curse on the whole town. I can't understand how Mrs. Gartini can take it seriously. She claims she watches it because it's so ridiculous. But if I reached up and changed the channel now she'd stab me in the heart.

"Well," I said when a commercial came on, "it's nice to know who your friends really are."

"Listen to me, Shepherd! I will give you a job! You can start today."

"There's no tape deck in the stockroom."

"We'll hire an orchestra! What do you want?"

I want to be thirty and rich and successful. I want to drive a red turbo Porsche. I want to live on my own in a penthouse apartment, with lots of nice furniture, and no lawn to mow.

But none of that is happening and it probably never will.

"Oh, here's Sheila now," Mrs. Gartini said.

Sheila swaggered up to the counter, grinning.

23

She's small and wiry with slick swimmer's hair. She spends more time in the water than a shark. We've known each other since kindergarten. It's never been a love affair.

"How's it going, Youngman?"

"Just fine," I said.

"Enjoying the summer?"

"Sure."

Those were the words you heard, but our eyes were saying something else.

"Shepherd may be working here too," Mrs. Gartini said. "Oh my, now Roger's had a heart attack and Melanie still doesn't know about Jeremy. That's what I love about this show; it's one stupid thing after another, just like life."

I graciously helped Sheila load the station wagon, over her strenuous objections.

"Listen," I said, stacking groceries in the back, "this was my job. I had it nailed."

"Apparently not." Sheila jingled the car keys. The sound lacerated my brain.

"Mrs. G. said I could have the job! I practically grew up in this store!"

It was true. She and my mother would yak for hours while I sucked Tootsie Pops and read comic books. "We'll leave in just a minute, Shep," my mother would promise. By the time they'd finished their conversations, I'd gone into a new shoe size.

"You don't have your license," Sheila said. "Case closed."

"You're too small to lift the groceries! I'm twice as big as you!"

Sheila flexed her bare arms. Muscles swam beneath the skin. She got into the car and slid a tape into the player. A band I hate blared in my ears.

"See ya, Shep." Sheila drove off in my station wagon. This was worse than a nightmare. This was real.

I went home. There was nothing to eat; just milk, bread, salad stuff, and a jar of spiced crab apples somebody gave us years ago. We never eat them and we don't throw them away. We're saving them for an emergency. Like a nuclear war.

It was only four o'clock. I had a baby-sitting job coming up that night for a kid like a crazed ferret, with teeth to match. I wasn't in the mood to deal with a brat. If he bit me again, I'd bite back.

It seemed like everything was going to hell, like I was living in the Haunted Village; just when things can't get worse, they do. I watched some stupid game show on TV. If I was a losing contestant, I wouldn't be a good sport. I'd punch the winner and strangle the host.

I went into my room. It's really depressing. There are posters on the ceiling from when I was a kid; baskets of puppies and kittens. The posters of rock stars look fakey and old. I don't listen to most of those groups anymore. The bookshelves are crammed with every book I've ever owned, including the ones I'd gnawed on. I lay down on my bed. The mattress is crummy. I felt like the poster boy for terminal boredom.

This is Shepherd. Other children can run and laugh and play. But Shepherd can't. Because, you see, Shepherd is bored. Please help. Send your contributions and car keys today—

My mother came in from work, juggling groceries. "How was your day, honey?"

"Terrible," I said, collapsing at the kitchen table.

"Why?"

I didn't feel like going into the details. "No reason. It just stank."

"Oh, Shepherd, can't you be in a good mood for once?"

"You asked me how my day was and I'm telling you."

"Jack's coming over for dinner tonight. Would you please make the salad?"

"I can't," I said. "I'm cleaning my room."

"You were supposed to clean your room this morning. Did you do the wash?"

"Not yet."

"Did you change the budgie's cage?"

"I'm going to," I said.

My mother slammed a zucchini on the counter. "I told you to clean his cage this morning! His seed cups are empty. He can't ask you for food."

"Why not? Budgies can talk."

Ours doesn't. He just screams and squawks and tries to peck your hand. His name is Conway Tweetie. He's way older than budgies usually get. He's like the Budgie That Time Forgot.

"When are you going to assume some responsibility?" My mother was warming up. "You want all the privileges, like driving a car, but you can't even do the wash!"

"What's the wash got to do with driving a car?"

"You just turn on the water and add the soap. It's not like operating a spaceship, you know. You're not a baby, Shepherd. You should do more housework. When are you going to start ironing your shirts?"

"I took out the garbage."

"Congratulations!"

"You're the one who's in a bad mood," I said, "just because you had a lousy day at work."

"I'm not talking about work! You didn't do your chores! Who was your maid last year?"

And so forth. We got dinner ready. I started the wash, watered the lawn, and changed the budgie's cage. He bit me.

Jack showed up and kissed my mother. That's the first time he's done that in front of me. The other day Ma was talking about having a baby; saying she might like to have another one sometime. That blew my mind. Are you kidding? I'd said. Lots of people my age have babies, she'd replied. Yeah, I'd said, but not you.

"How's it going, Shep?" Jack asked.

"Okay."

"Having fun this summer?"

"No."

For some reason, he and my mother laughed. That really annoyed me.

"Well, school will be starting soon," he said, completely missing the point.

My mother broke out the potato chips and clam dip. "We'll eat pretty soon," she said.

I went out into the driveway and shot some hoops. In a while Jack came out and said, "Mind if I join you?" My mother was right behind him. Does she come out and watch me when I'm by myself? No.

I tossed the ball in the garage. "I've got to get going. I'm sitting for the Morrisons tonight."

"But you haven't had dinner," Ma said.

"I'll eat there. See you later." I got on my bike and hit the road.

My mother said something; she called my name, but I didn't turn around, I kept going.

C H A P T E R
F I V E

My father was supposed
to come and get me, but I ended up taking the bus.

He called just before he was due to arrive. "I can't
get away from the club," he said. "You'll have to meet
me here."

My mother wasn't pleased. She wanted to give me
a ride to the city but I insisted that wasn't necessary.

"It only takes an hour to get there, Ma. What could
happen on the bus?"

She imagines a world of kidnappers and hijackers,
scheming to snatch her baby son. She grumbled as
she drove me to the bus station.

"Your father," she began, then changed her mind.
"Did you pack your pajamas?"

"I have my pajamas."

"And your toothbrush and slippers and the clothes
for the reunion?"

"Check and double check."

She parked the car. "Here's some money for the ticket and a taxi when you get there, and some quarters in case you need to make a phone call."

Don't forget the lead weights, in case you go fishing. And your flame-retardant underpants, in case there's a fire. She waited by the car while I bought a ticket, then gave me a big hug and kiss.

"Take care of yourself, bunny."

"I'm not a bunny."

"Call me when you get there so I'll know you arrived. Have a good time!"

She stood there and waved as the bus pulled away. It looked like she was trying not to cry.

The bus ride was uneventful except for the usual space cadet, who sat in the seat beside me; a young guy with wild eyes and a woolly beard garnished with scrambled eggs. He was talking about The Conspiracy.

"You know which one I mean, don't you?" he asked me.

"Sure," I said, pretending to be entranced with the passing scenery.

"There's lots of conspiracies but they're all the same one. It's a conglomeration of the military-industrial complex and General Foods. Have you ever had Wheaties? I've seen the files. I used to be in advertising."

He kept this up all the way to the city. At the bus station there were hundreds of guys just like him. I guess they were having a convention.

I took a cab with the money Ma gave me. It dropped me off in front of my father's club. It's called "The Laugh Track." The location's not bad; there were only a *few* winos hanging around outside.

I walked into the bar. It was dark and almost empty. The bartender looked up and said, "Beat it, sonny. This ain't the Y."

"It's okay, it's my kid." Joey materialized. He introduced me to the bartender.

"Frank, this is Shepherd. Shepherd, Frank."

"How you doing, Shep?" Frank asked.

"Okay."

My father reached behind me and tugged my braid. "You're going to get this thing caught in a door someday."

"Don't start." I moved away from him.

"Okay, okay, I can take a hint. Come on, I want to show you around."

The main room was good-sized. The chairs and tables were slick and new. There was a little stage up front with some lights aimed at it. Down the hall were the kitchen and some offices and dressing rooms, and a storeroom where they kept the booze.

"Like it?" Joey said. You could tell he was proud.

"Sure."

31

"Business has been really good. Hey, I'm sorry I couldn't come get you tonight but this thing came up. It's business all the time, but I ain't complaining. Sit down. Do you want a soda or something?"

We sat down in Joey's office and I drank a soda and he had a drink and smoked a cigarette. He was sitting behind a big blond desk. I bet all the drawers were empty.

He was looking pretty cute, as *People* Magazine said, with his hair brushed back and fluffy as a puppy's, and jeans and a white shirt with rainbow suspenders. The article said women want to mother him.

Smother him, they mean, Ma's friend Jane said. She saw the article at our house the other night. Jane's known us since I was a baby and Joey left. She thinks he's a clown, the joke of the century, for leaving us in the lurch.

Once when I was small, I lost a helium balloon. The string slipped through my fingers. I tried to reach it but it floated away. I watched it for a long time, until it finally disappeared. That's kind of what happened with my father.

"So, Shep!" Joey said, leaning back in his chair. "I meant to get back to you sooner but things have been pretty hectic. Wait till you see the apartment. It's fantastic. There's a chance I could buy the building."

"Are you rich?" It seemed like a fair question.

He laughed. "You've got to be kidding. But I've got connections. I know a lot of people, Sport, and I want you to know them too. I've been doing a lot of thinking about me and you."

I knew what was coming. I've seen it happen with my friends. Daddy suddenly has an attack of the guilts. It's like they wake up one day and say: I *knew* I was forgetting something! My kid! They want to take you to baseball games and go fishing; all the stuff that would've meant a lot when you were little.

"I want us to get to really know each other," Joey said. "We've never had the chance to spend time together."

"That's because you went away," I said. "You could've stayed in Santa Rosa."

"And done what? Sold Kinney shoes at the mall? Gotten a job in a gas station?"

"Those aren't the only jobs in the world," I said. "You didn't have to be a comedian."

Joey leaned toward me, blowing smoke out of his nose. "Listen," he said, "I'm not Ward Cleaver, and I'm never going to be, okay? Your mother got pregnant. That wasn't in the program. What was I supposed to do, hang up all my dreams? Say: 'Well, I guess that's the end for me?' I was just a baby."

"So was I."

Joey leaned back in his chair. We glared at each

33

other. He shook his head and said, "I don't understand you."

"Of course you don't. You don't even know me."

"I know you're my kid, my flesh and blood. We've finally got the chance to spend time together. This club's going to work out good. I'll be around. I know I haven't been the best father in the world—hey, give me a break. Don't make that face. You look just like your mother. What do you want me to do, cry blood?"

"I don't want you to do anything," I said.

"Oh, fine." Joey ground out his cigarette, scowling.

Someone knocked at the door, then a woman stuck her head in.

"Joey, Ray Vaughn's out front."

"Okay, I'll be right there. Gina, this is my son, Shepherd. See if he needs something, will you?" Joey left.

Gina was pretty with long dark hair. I wondered who she was. The hostess? My new stepmother? It turned out she was another bartender. She didn't seem to know what to do with me. She brought me some fancy appetizers and gave me a *Chronicle* to read. The food tasted good but you couldn't tell what it was; it was all dressed up.

I remembered to call my mother. I used the phone on Joey's desk. She answered in half a ring.

"How's it going, honey?"

"Just peachy," I told her.

She said, "Don't forget to floss your teeth."

I roamed around the club for a while but it was beginning to fill up. Joey was busy talking to people, making them laugh, buying them drinks.

People like Joey. They think he's really friendly. He's not; he's just making them laugh. It's a power trip. He likes to pull the strings. *Remember, Sport, a smile is mostly teeth.*

The club got full and the talk was real loud. There was music playing too. If you just listened to the noise, it didn't sound human. A lot of the people were much younger than Joey; yupsters, he calls them in his act; with lots of bucks to spend on clothes and cars and overpriced food and booze. I watched Gina for a while. She didn't just mix drinks, she juggled the bottles like an acrobat.

Joey walked onstage to warm up the crowd and introduce the first comedian. He got a big round of applause. "Isn't that nice?" he said. "What a good-looking group! And so young! I hope you got all your homework done before you came down here to-night."

He got the crowd rolling. It didn't matter what he said; they wanted to laugh and they did, on cue. Even when Joey's jokes are stupid, his timing is good. He delivers each line like a big gorgeous present he's picked out just for you.

"Before we start the show—and we've got some great talent tonight—I want to introduce the most important person in my life . . . me. No, what? My hairstylist? Oh, do you like my do? I look like what? A cockapoo? Honey, is that a compliment, or are you cussing me out? Do your parents know you're here? We'll try to get you home before curfew. Anyway! I want you to meet my son, Shepherd. Shep, stand up and let everybody take a look at you!"

But I was long gone, down the hall.

I went back to Joey's office and finished the *Chronicle*. There was a phone book and some old magazines in one of the desk drawers. The rest were locked.

I thumbed through an ancient *Life* magazine and read about the happy marriage of two movie stars, now divorced. At the back of the magazine was a black-and-white photograph of a hand holding a tiny monkey's paw.

The words beneath the picture said the hand belonged to a priest. But it wasn't a paw resting in his palm; it was the hand of a starving, dying African kid.

I kept looking at that photograph. It made me feel awful. I put the magazine back in the drawer. Gina brought me some ginger ale and peanuts, and *People* magazine, in case I hadn't seen it.

"We're all pretty proud of your dad," she said, as if expecting me to agree.

I read the article again, just to make sure. It didn't mention me. Most of the stories written about Joey don't include his phantom family.

The article was called "Forever Young! The Kid's Still Kidding Around!" The picture showed Joey jumping into the air, his arms and legs spread wide.

According to the writer, "Joey (34) has never been hotter, with nightclub appearances, his own comedy club, and a possible TV show." As I read, I kept seeing that terrible picture—the tiny dying hand shriveled down to nothing. Meanwhile, here's Joey and his trendy fans, stuffing themselves with designer appetizers and yukking it up at a bunch of stupid jokes.

Joey doesn't do political humor. He says people have enough problems; they just want to be entertained.

I'd fallen asleep, my head on his desk, by the time he came looking for me.

"How'd you like the show?" he asked in the car.

"Fine." No sense telling him I hadn't seen it. "I got tired."

"Hang on. We're almost home."

He parked the Galaxie in a garage beneath the building. We took the elevator to the top, the fourth floor. Joey unlocked the door and started turning on lights. The apartment was huge, with lots of windows and a terrific view of the Bay Bridge. Even late at night it was streaming with headlights. I wondered where everyone was going.

"Look at this," Joey said. "It's a collector's item." He was pointing at a coffee table in front of the white couch. The glass top was balanced on a naked, kneeling woman's back. My mother would've thrown it out the window.

"It's by the same guy who did those," Joey said proudly, indicating two huge paintings that could've been done by a kindergarten class. "They're an investment," he added. "Want something to eat, Sport?"

We went into the kitchen. Everything in there was shiny and new. "A gal comes in twice a week," Joey said.

And does what? Cleans? Or kneels in the living room, serving drinks?

"I'm pretty tired. I think I'll go to bed," I said.

Joey looked disappointed. He was wide awake. "I'll show you your room," he said.

"That's okay. I'll just sleep on the couch."

"What for? I got you a bed."

"Why?"

"To sleep in. Duh. What do you think I do with houseguests? Stack them in the closet at night?" Joey said.

I followed him down the hall. There were two johns, one off his room, one off mine. I'd never had a bathroom to myself before. Joey's room was the size of a football field, and white, with an enormous bed and a mirrored closet running along one wall. My room was a slightly smaller version of Joey's. Everything in it was the color of the snow.

"How do you like it?" Joey asked.

"It's fine."

"That's all you can say? It's fine? Do you have any idea how much this stuff cost?"

"Dad, you sound like a game show host."

Joey looked annoyed then he let it go. "I keep forgetting you're a kid," he said.

"Yeah, I know."

"You can hang up your clothes in the closet, if you want."

"This is all I have." I held my duffel bag.

"You brought something nice for the reunion, right? And a hairnet too, I hope."

"Don't take me, if you don't want to. This was your idea, not mine," I said.

"Geez, you're such a grouch!"

"It's two o'clock in the morning!"

"So go to bed. We'll leave around noon. Goodnight."

"Good night," I said, and closed the door in his

face. He was standing there like he was expecting a tip. What did he want me to do, hug him?

I was really tired but I couldn't fall asleep. The sheets were too new; they crackled. I felt like a letter in an envelope. Dear Dad, this won't work. It's hopeless.

I kept seeing that picture, that tiny little hand. Then I told myself: It was an old magazine. That baby isn't hungry anymore.

C H A P T E R
S I X

When I woke up, I didn't notice it was gone. I was confused; where was I? The room was so white I thought I'd died and gone to heaven.

God, are you there?

I'm here, Shepherd. How are you?

Just fine, Lord. And you?

Couldn't be better.

Well, actually, Lord, I'm not too fine. I think I died during the night.

Are you sure, Shepherd? I don't see your name on the list.

The light is so bright here. It hurts my eyes.

You're in Joey's apartment, in San Francisco.

Oh, yeah ... I have to go to his reunion today. I don't know why he wants me to go.

He's proud of you, Shepherd. He wants to show you off.

Joey can show off just fine by himself.

Shepherd, be nice. Don't hurt his feelings.

Why is everybody so worried about his feelings? I have feelings too!

Of course you do. You're a fine young man. Joey may not show it, but he needs your love.

He's not a child, Lord.

Neither are you. You're wise beyond your years, Shepherd.

Thanks, God. Same to you.

I got out of bed. My toes sank into the carpet. Sunlight was pouring into the room.

Joey was on the phone in the living room. He pointed me toward the kitchen and said, "I don't care what he says. You tell the boys at the network..."

I ate some English muffins and had a cup of coffee with lots of milk.

Joey finally got off the phone and came into the kitchen. "How'd you sleep?" he asked.

"On my stomach," I said.

"You better take a shower and get dressed. We're running late. There's shampoo in the tub."

I went into the bathroom and brushed my teeth. The guy in the mirror looked unfamiliar. I couldn't put my finger on what was different.

Then I realized my braid was gone.

Just gone. Like an idiot I kept feeling my head; it had to be there, maybe in my ear. It was like the time our stereo was stolen. I kept going back to the place where it was supposed to be; like it had to be there, but it must be invisible.

I went into the living room.

"You bastard," I said.

Joey smiled and shrugged, embarrassed.

"How could you do that? You had no right! It's my hair! You shouldn't have done that!"

"You're right," Joey said. "You're right. I'm sorry. But you look so terrific without it, Shep. You can't even tell it's missing."

"I can tell it's missing!" I had never been so mad at him. "Where is it?"

"What're you going to do? Glue it back on?"

"Give me my damn hair!"

"I don't have it," he said. "It's in the trash."

It was in the garbage can under the sink, curled up like a little brown snake. Stuff was sticking to it. I started to rinse it off. Then I felt like I was holding something dead. I dropped it in the trash can and went into the bathroom and slammed and locked the door.

Joey knocked gently. "Shep, I'm sorry."

"Go away. I'm not talking to you anymore."

"It was stupid of me. It was kind of a joke."

"A joke!" I shouted. "That's a laugh!"

"I just thought you'd look so good. When I was your age I would've given a million bucks to look like you. But I didn't; I was a fat little shrimp. I'm sorry, Sport. What can I say. I'm an idiot."

I turned on the shower so I wouldn't have to hear him. Hot water rained on my skin. The hell with the reunion. I wasn't going to go. Joey thinks he can do anything he wants and everybody will always forgive him.

When I came out he was standing in the living room, looking out at the Bay Bridge. He turned around. There were tears in his eyes. He said, "Sport, can you ever forgive me? You're right. I was wrong. I had no business doing that. You're not a little boy anymore. I just want you to get the best out of life. I don't want people putting you down. You believe me, don't you? I acted like a moron. I hope you can find it in your heart to forgive me."

So why did I end up going to the reunion? Joey was right; he'd acted like a moron. But he's *my* moron. He's all I've got. He's my dad.

We drove to Sacramento in the Galaxie. I rolled down my window so I wouldn't have to breathe his cigarette smoke. He was acting like everything was hunky-dory. I was still so mad I couldn't look at him, but Joey didn't notice.

"Am I glad to be out of L.A.!" he said, tailgating at seventy. "I'm telling you, it's another planet down there. The people are so phony. You never know who's going to stab you in the back.

"I met my agent for lunch in this ritzy part of town. All these big hotels. You can't believe the money down there. Meanwhile, the sidewalks are swarming with bums; homeless people, just wandering around. They sleep in the parks at night. I guess. I don't know where the hell they sleep but you see them every day.

"So I go to the hotel where the restaurant is. There's a glass elevator going up the side of the building; all the windows are mirrors. Pretty spiffy. I'm standing on the sidewalk, looking up at this thing; it looks like the headquarters for heaven. Then I start smelling this really weird smell. I look down and I'm standing next to a pile of crap! These people just go in the bushes, you know. Talk about perspective! It was hilarious."

Joey grew up in Sacramento. When he graduated from high school, he split. He hardly ever goes back to see his family. He and his dad never got along, and he's not close to his brother or sister. When I was a kid I used to wish I had a brother, but it's not the kind of thing you find under the Christmas tree.

The reunion was being held in a city park; an afternoon get-together so people could bring their families, followed by a dinner and dance, at the Holiday Inn. It was the first reunion Joey had attended. I could tell he was nervous. He kept smoking and blabbing.

"Weird, isn't it, Shep?" he said as we pulled into the city. "I perform in front of strangers all the time, get up and make a fool of myself on TV, but this thing is different. It's getting to me. I haven't seen these guys in twenty years and it's like yesterday, you know? They used to make me feel so lousy."

"Then why are you going?"

"Good question." Joey lit another cigarette. "I guess it's time to get this thing out of my system; lay a few ghosts to rest. Also, I want to see how some of these jerks made out. I'm the only one in our class who's famous. Well, not like the president or Elvis, you know, but you understand what I'm saying. I'll tell you what success is," he said as if I'd asked. "Success is when you go into a four-star restaurant, anywhere, New York, L.A., Vegas, and you get the best table, no questions asked."

I said, "How do you know if the people really like you or if they're just kissing your ass?"

"What difference does it make? You get the table. Trouble is, somebody's always crawling up your back. Some hot new talent. They come around, acting like your biggest fan: Let me study at your feet. That kind of thing. But they just want to stand on your head."

"Sounds wonderful," I said.

"It is." Joey laughed. "As long as you're the one on top."

46

We parked the car near a big open field. At the far end there were lots of people and picnic tables and balloons. Joey got out of the car, brushing his hair back with his fingers. He lit a cigarette. I was tying my shoes.

"Come on, will you, Shep?" I almost laughed, he was so antsy. But Joey doesn't like people laughing at him except when he wants them to.

We approached the crowd. The people looked old. "It looks like the wax museum," I said. "Or some kind of retirement center."

"Geez," Joey muttered, "Scott Dawson's so fat! And he's either wearing a rug or he's got a hamster on his head."

The next thing I knew people were rushing up to Joey, clapping him on the back and shaking his hand.

"Hello, you old son of a gun!" Joey kept saying. "I can't believe it! Is that really you?"

People were wearing name tags featuring their pictures from the high school yearbook. At first I thought they were pictures of their kids. A lot of the guys were heavy and the women were blond and tan. There were lots of little kids there and a few my age. I talked to a kid named Luke from San Francisco. My hand kept going to the back of my head, feeling for the hair that wasn't there.

The adults were drinking beer and wine. Joey's nervousness had evaporated. He was working the

47

crowd the way a farmer milks cows. You could practically hear the mooing.

He was making jokes and telling people about his TV show, adding some details I hadn't heard. It sounded as if the show was going to start filming any second; like it was already listed in *TV Guide*.

You would've thought Joey was voted most popular in his class. Everybody seemed to know him and want to say hello, except for a few guys who hung back, looking jealous. Women swarmed around him, kissing and hugging him; their shiny red mouths open, ready to laugh.

Finally Joey hunted me up and said it was time to go to our motel, so he could clean up for the dinner dance. He said I could hang out there and watch TV while he was gone.

I said, "Maybe I'll go see Gram and Grampa."

Joey stopped for a traffic signal and punched in the cigarette lighter. He looked doubtful. "That'd be kind of complicated," he said.

"They could come and get me."

"I don't think that would work out." Translation: Forget it. He'd have to pick me up there and he didn't want to see them.

"That's okay," I said. "I'll just watch TV."

"No way," Joey said. "You can come with me. You can be my date for the evening."

I didn't want to do that. I said I'd be fine. But Joey had had a little wine and he was playing the great father. Besides, he was afraid I'd call them while he was gone, and he didn't want to risk a scene.

We took showers at the motel and I turned on the TV. There was a movie on later I wanted to see, a comedy with Rodney Dangerfield.

"I've seen it," Joey said, patting on aftershave. "It's a bomb. Did I tell you I met Dangerfield? An arrogant ███. That's the trouble with this business; it squeezes you dry. By the time you make it, you're so ████ off that when you get onstage all you want to say is: ████ you! And if you're Dangerfield or Eddie Murphy, people lap it up. It's ridiculous."

The TV filled the room. Joey likes to have noise going. We watched a cable comedy special. Joey had fun taking the acts apart.

When a commercial came on, he remembered I was there. He said, "You know what the trouble is with you and me, Shep? We're on different wavelengths. You remind me a lot of your mother."

"That's a shock. I've only lived with her for fifteen years."

"She's so ████ serious all the time."

"No, she's not," I said. "Just when she's talking to you."

The weird thing is, I remind her of him. She says,

You haven't been around him, but you have his mannerisms; the way you hold your head, and talk. It's spooky. It's spooky, all right.

Another comedian came on, a woman. Joey wasn't interested. He thinks women aren't funny.

"You don't understand the world I live in," he continued. "I mean, here I am, thirty-five years old—"

"No you're not," I said. "You're the same age as the people at the reunion."

"Thirty-five, forty—that's not the point. The point is, you see these losers on the tube. I mean, look at the woman. That's funny? Talking about her kids. Who cares about that stuff? They make funny faces or talk like Porky Pig, and they're the ones who get a shot at the big time."

"You used to do Elmer Fudd," I said.

"Are you listening to me? The point is this: I'm looking down the road and what do I see? *Old* Joey Young, making jokes on a cruise ship or working a bar for drinks; the headliner at supermarket openings. So what do I do? Do I bail out now, or do I keep hanging in? I mean, sometimes these things take time. Look at Dangerfield. The cat's been around."

I always think Joey will want to know about me; what do I like, what do I want to do with my life. But the questions don't occur to him. I'm his straight man.

I put on my good clothes ("You're wearing those?"

he said) and we drove to the Holiday Inn. There were hundreds of people there, all dressed up. I felt out of place; I saw one other kid my age. She looked like she was considering divorcing her parents.

After a while I could've taken off my clothes and nobody would've noticed. They were drinking and smoking and laughing real loud. There was music playing too, twenty years old. People would run up to each other and shriek: "You look so great!" They'd hug each other, then spin away. It was all hellos and good-byes.

Dinner was okay; some kind of chicken with rice and vegetables. We were supposed to get dessert too but it never arrived. Some guy came by our table with a video camera and Joey hammed it up. Point a lens at him and he goes bananas.

A woman had attached herself to my father. She was pretty and blond with a shiny tan. Her name was Nancy. She kept smiling at me and she told my father I was darling.

People danced for a while; then some guy got up and handed out awards, for the most kids, the youngest child, the most marriages and divorces. Then somebody shouted, "Joey, get up and say something! Come on, Joey!" People at our table took up the chant.

"I can't," Joey said, smiling. "Come on, you guys."

He said it all the way to the stage. Nancy squeezed my hand, her eyes sparkling. "Isn't this exciting?" she said.

Joey tapped the microphone. "Can you hear me? Nod your heads. Some of you were nodding when you got here, right? The night is young but we're not. I got here tonight, I thought it was a retirement center. The wax museum! I'm not kidding! I, however, was a precocious child and was only ten years old when I graduated. You don't believe me? Would this baby face lie?"

Nancy leaned close and whispered, "Isn't he great? How can he make up this stuff on the spot?"

He didn't. Joey had gone over some notes at the motel, just in case they asked him to wing it.

"High school," Joey sighed. "Who can ever forget it? The brain cells are dying. That's a help. Some of you tall guys probably remember me from basketball. I was the basket."

The people laughed and clapped.

"I wanted to fit in so badly!" Joey said. "And not just in lockers and trash cans. Finally—and this was the greatest day of my life—I was chosen to be the mascot for the Carlton High Chipmunks. You should've seen me! I was so proud! So I report to the coach and ask for my costume—he hands me some nuts for my cheeks!

"What? It wasn't the Chipmunks? The Cougars, huh? See, high school was such a drag for me that a few years ago I had this surgical procedure where they give you a new memory. So now I remember being tall and tough and hunky—What? Instead of short, fat, and wimpy? See what I mean! The only thing that kept me going in high school was knowing that someday I'd get my revenge. It was like I thought everybody else would get old and fat and ugly while I stayed incredibly young and beautiful. And I was right!

"But, hey, who has time to hold a grudge these days? We've all got exes and bills and kids. My kid drove here with me today. Hates my smoking. I mean absolutely hates it! He's got his head out the window like a German shepherd! He says, 'Dad, smoking's going to kill you!' What isn't? If I jog, do I get eternal life? No, I get shin splints!"

I left when he started joking about my braid. I went outside and hung around the pool. A man and a woman were swimming in it. It was lit inside and glittered like a jewel.

After a long time Joey came and got me. The blond woman was hanging on his arm.

"Ready to go, Sport?"

I didn't say a thing. I followed them out to the parking lot and got into the backseat.

We didn't give Nancy a ride home; she came back to our motel. Joey stopped by the office then he let her into our room. "I'll be right there, Nance," he said and closed the door. He and I were standing outside.

"Sport, can I talk to you for a minute?" he said. I hate that Sport stuff. I was fuming. "Nancy's going to spend the night. I've got you another room. Here's the key."

"What?" I looked at the key in my hand.

"It's just two doors down. You don't mind, do you, Shep? We're going to do some heavy reminiscing, if you catch my meaning."

I boiled over. I said, "You are such a jerk."

"What're you talking about?"

"You're unbelievable! We come up here today— You act like such a chump, telling everybody all this stuff! And now you pick her up! Have you heard of safe sex? What about the AIDS epidemic?"

Joey looked at me like I was nuts. He said, "I hate to tell you this, you little idiot, but Nancy's no hooker drug addict."

I said, "I hate to tell you this, you little idiot, but what's that got to do with it? You don't even know her!"

"Will you keep your voice down? I've got condoms with me."

"Oh, that's just terrific. That's great! Mighty Joey

Young comes prepared for anything: sex, jokes—"

"What's the matter with you? Why are you acting like a baby?"

"I'm not acting like a baby!" I was crying. "You do that phony stuff: me and my son, the teenager. Like I'm really your son! Like you're really my dad! You just steal what I say and put it in your act! It's all an act! The whole damn thing!"

"Lower your voice," Joey said. "I mean it."

"Why did you bring me? You don't even like me! Now you're just going to dump me!"

"For God's sake, Shepherd, I'm not marrying the woman. We're just sleeping together. It's no big deal."

"You don't understand a thing I say!"

"Not when you don't make sense."

Nancy opened the door. Her smile was quivering. "Is anything wrong?" she asked.

It wasn't her fault. I felt sorry for her. Something inside me collapsed.

"Nothing's wrong," Joey said. "I'll be right there."

Nancy closed the door. I told my father, "I'm going to go see Gram and Grampa."

"When? Tonight?"

"Yes."

"It's too late."

"So what? They won't care. They'll be glad to see me."

"No," Joey said. "I'll take you over there tomorrow."

"That's a lie. Anyway, you can't stop me. I'm leaving."

"Let's get something straight," Joey said, his face mean. "You don't talk to me like that. I'm running the show. You're the kid, I'm the dad."

"Since when?"

"I give up." He looked disgusted. "You do what you want. I'll see you."

He went into his room and locked the door. I stood there, feeling like I was going crazy.

Gram and Grampa would come and take me to their house. They'd hug me and they'd want me to stay. But they'd be mad at Joey. Imagine him leaving you like that! they'd say. It would be a real festival; Slam-Dunk Joey Day. You'd think I'd enjoy that but I don't. I'd end up doing what I always do; covering for him. It's no big deal, I'd say. After a while I'd almost mean it.

I went into my room and stayed up late, watching the Dangerfield movie. It wasn't funny. I wondered if he had any kids.

In the morning I had breakfast with my father and Nancy. She smiled at me a lot. He seemed depressed, but he perked up when the waitress recognized him.

We dropped Nancy off at her apartment. She said, "Now don't forget to call me."

"I won't," Joey said. "See you at the next reunion."

She laughed. I guess she thought he was kidding.

We didn't talk much on the way home. "I'll be in touch," he said as I got out of the car, then he drove off. I went inside.

Ma hugged me. "How was it? Did you have a good time?" Then she said, "Honey, what happened to your braid?"

"It's gone? You're kidding!" I grabbed the back of my neck. "Somebody must've swiped it!"

My father would've been proud of me.

CHAPTER
SEVEN

It was odd to be back in school. The summer seemed like a handful of snapshots, glanced through then scattered and lost.

Everybody talked about what they'd done on vacation; they'd gone to Disneyland, Hawaii, the Alps. I didn't have much to brag about. What could I say? That I baby-sat and gave the budgie a bath? A lot of tenth-graders were driving cars. I had all kinds of room in the bike racks.

As usual, for the beginning of school, my schedule was screwed up. I had a couple of classes I didn't want and didn't have a couple I needed. My locker wouldn't open. The librarian informed me that I still hadn't turned in a book from last year. The smell from the cafeteria wafted through the halls. Today's special: barbecued tires.

Sheila the She-Monster was in my math class. Swampy was sitting behind me. He poked me in the back and said, "I need a favor."

Mr. Munson barked, "Youngman, turn around."

"I was just—"

"Save it!" Mr. Munson thundered. I had him last year too, and I wasn't his favorite.

Swampy whispered, "I've got a cash flow problem."

His problem is, it's always flowing out. His parents are loaded and they give him lots of dough, but he blows it on clothes, tapes, and his car. For a while he was into coke, but now he's not.

I'm not into dope. I smoked some weed one time, but it made me feel like I was floating away. I like to stay in control. Besides, when I get money I don't want to set it on fire and inhale it.

I turned around and said, "I'll talk to you later."

"I'm warning you, Youngman!" Mr. Munson shouted. It was only the end of the first week of school and I was dancing on the edge of detention. He said, "Perhaps you'd like to teach the class, since you seem to have so much to say."

"No, thanks."

"Then pay attention. That goes for the rest of you. We're here to learn, not to visit with our friends. Perhaps we need to review the progression of penalties I've outlined on the blackboard. Youngman, why don't you read it to the class. You know how to read, don't you?"

"There's no need to be sarcastic," I said.

Mr. Munson's eyeballs bulged. The lines in his face looked like they'd been carved with an ax. "I'll hang you from the flagpole, if I feel like it!" he said. He's the kind of guy who believes in capital punishment—in the classroom. When he's really wound up he calls us cheeseheads.

I read the notice in chalk aloud: "Disrupting the class: talking, laughing, et cetera—first warning. Second warning: detention. Third warning: sent to the office and a note sent home. Fourth warning: one-day suspension."

Fifth warning: death by firing squad. Mr. Munson stomps around the front of the room in high black boots, freshly licked. He wears a crisp uniform and a helmet shaped like a wedge of cheddar. He carries a small whip, which he cracks in the air, punctuating each sentence:

"Listen, you cheeseheads," he hisses. "You will do what I tell you. And you'll do it fast, with no backtalk, is that clear?"

"Yes, Mr. Munson," Sheila simpers. He whips out a Luger and shoots her.

"No backtalk, I said! You're not listening!" he screams. "You are here to learn! Open your books!"

Swampy raises a hand. "Can I ask a question?"

"No!" Another shot rings out. Swampy slumps across his desk. "I'm going to squeeze some algebra into your fat little cheeseheads if it's the last thing I do! Do you hear me?"

"I said, do you hear me, Youngman?" Mr. Munson towered above me.

"Yes," I said. "I read you loud and clear."

Swampy nabbed me in the hall after class. His clothes and his haircut were new. He looks like an ad for Neiman-Marcus for the first few weeks of school.

"Thanks for almost getting me killed," I said. We went into the quad. Rock music was blasting. That's supposed to be our big lunchtime treat.

"I've got a problem," Swampy said. He looked wigged out. A bunch of our friends went by. They were going across the street to eat at the Hi-Fi.

"Go ahead," I told Ryan. "We'll be right there."

"I was wondering if I could borrow some money," Swampy said. His eyes looked funny. They were darting around.

"What for? Dope?"

"No way," he said, as if the idea had never occurred to him. "It's for these phone calls I was making. The bill came yesterday. My folks are going to kill me when they see it."

"Who were you calling?"

"The Party Line." Swampy smiled, embarrassed.

I said, "You're kidding."

The Party Line is this rip-off deal where you pay a lot of money to talk to strangers. The ads on TV call it "a great way to meet new friends!" Sure, if you enjoy chatting with a bunch of losers.

"How much do you owe?"

"Not that much. Three hundred and twenty-eight dollars. See, I met this girl and she sounded real cute—"

"Are you crazy? I can't believe you'd do that."

"She sounded so cool. We'd talk for hours. Then all these other people would get on the line. She says I'm going to get to meet her soon. One time I asked her to come over to the house—"

I could've socked him. He goes around wearing this KICK ME sign, and then wonders why he's always black-and-blue.

"You shouldn't give out your address on the phone! You have no idea who's listening! Didn't you see that thing in the paper about this girl who called up and met this guy and she invited him over to the house? Then, when he gets there, he's not seventeen; he's thirty years old and he and his buddies raped her. And they stole a bunch of stuff—"

"I don't read the papers. They're too depressing," Swampy said. "Anyway, she's not that kind of person."

"You are really nuts."

Swampy looked ticked. "Are you going to help me or are you just going to insult me?"

"No, I can't help you. I don't have that kind of money. I've only got two hundred bucks in the bank and I'm saving that for car insurance."

"By the time you drive, you won't need a car. People will be wearing jetpacks," Swampy said. "Could you borrow it from your dad? He's rich."

"Your dad is the president of a bank!"

"Yeah, but your dad is real nice. Mine isn't."

"You don't even know Joey."

"But I've seen him on TV. I promise to pay you back."

"You never pay me back."

"This time I will."

"I'm sorry," I said, "but I can't."

"Some friend." Swampy turned around and walked away. He looked like a little kid.

My appetite was shot. I didn't go to the Hi-Fi. When the guys came back, Ryan said, "What's with Swampy?" I just shrugged. We've all hung out together since first grade. We're tight. But we don't blab about our problems. Talking about them doesn't help. It just makes the problems more real.

I didn't see Swampy again until seventh period. He wasn't making eye contact. Living Skills is not my favorite class. It's too much like a talk show, covering all the trendy topics of the day: AIDS, divorce, domestic violence. Welcome to the wonderful world of adulthood.

Mrs. Bloom divided us into groups so we could develop a topic to present to the class. Swampy was in my group, pretending I was invisible. Sheila was sitting across from me next to Lucia, a new girl from Santa Barbara with long dark hair and brown eyes. I tried to look at her, but every time I did, Sheila stared at me.

The only thing we were able to focus on was the clock. We couldn't agree on a topic. Mrs. Bloom told us that we were supposed to keep journals. Every day we had to write at least one paragraph describing the things that happened to us, and what we thought and felt. She was the only person who'd see what we'd written. As if I'd tell a teacher what I was thinking.

I went home after school. The mail was full of bills and a note for me from my father. Inside was a check for two hundred bucks. The note said, "For school clothes. I'll see you soon."

He's been buttering me up since the reunion. He's called a couple of times. Things are going good at the club and his TV show is about to start filming. I thought when it did he'd have to move to L.A., but they're going to shoot it in San Francisco.

"Lots of shows are shot here now," he said on the phone the other night. "And here's the beauty part—this is so fantastic, Shep—they're going to shoot it right here at the club! The show's about this comic who owns a comedy club—sound like anybody you know? So I can play myself, and have lots of special guests—"

"Maybe I could play your son," I said.

"Oh, the guy doesn't have a kid," Joey said. "But he has a dog that drives him nuts."

I could give the money Joey sent me to Swampy. Or I could give it to my mother to buy a new chair. The big one in the living room is totally disintegrating. When you sit in it to watch TV it feels like somebody's got a knife in your ribs.

It was a lot of money and not enough. I rode my bike to the bank and deposited it in my savings account. On the way home I saw some of the guys playing soccer, in the big field behind the gym. I didn't sign up this year because I thought I'd be working. I watched them scrimmage for a while. It felt weird not to be on the team.

I went home and got my school work done because there was a show on later I wanted to see. The math was easy. For English I had to read a chapter from Of Mice and Men. I could see myself as George and Swampy as Lenny.

The journal assignment for Mrs. Bloom's class was a problem. I turned the empty notebook over and over in my hands. This is what I could've written: Today sucked. Mr. Munson is a Nazi. He hates me. Swampy wants me to give him all my money. Sheila the She-Monster keeps sneering at me. I'd like to punch her in the face. Everyone I know has their license already or at least is taking driver's training. Ma won't let me drive till I'm eighty. I don't have a real job. I'm sick of mowing lawns and baby-sitting. My father sent me a bunch of money. He thinks he can buy me pretty cheap.

Instead, I wrote: Not much happened today. Went to school, went to the bank, went home, watched TV. My mother made meatloaf and macaroni for dinner. The stupid budgie bit me.

CHAPTER
EIGHT

I can always tell when Ma's been to see her counselor. She comes home chatty and optimistic. After her session Thursday night, she said she'd take me out to dinner. On our budget, that's a major event.

She'd put a new bumper sticker on the back of her old Dodge: "Since I gave up all hope, I feel much better!" I politely suggested that she take it off. She cheerfully recommended that I eat a brick. I hate riding in that car, it's an embarrassment. When I'm driving I'll get my own set of wheels, something powerful and shiny and new.

We went to a Chinese restaurant downtown. Ma ordered plum wine. I drank tea.

"So, how's school going, bunny?"

"The name is Shepherd."

"I know what your name is. I named you that my-self. But you'll always be my little bunny."

"No, I won't. Your little bunny's dead. I ran over him with the lawn mower."

"Shepherd, don't be such a twit," she said pleas-antly. The waitress brought us bowls of soup filled with pale mysterious chunks. Tofu? Shark? The cook's thumbs? "Did anything interesting happen at school today?"

"No." Mr. Munson had almost killed me again but that wasn't what she wanted to hear. The last few weeks of school haven't gone too smoothly. Adults can call you a cheesehead and get away with it, but if I say one thing back, he throws a fit. I know I should keep my mouth shut but I can't. When I hear the kids laughing, it goes to my head.

"Did you fill out those sweepstakes forms?" she asked me.

"Yeah. They're in the mail." We have a deal. She doesn't have time to figure out the Amalgamated Magazine Money Marathon Sweepstakes entries, so I complete the forms, and if we win the prize, we'll split it. Since we never order any magazines, they probably throw our entry away. Which reminds me: I better hide that *Playboy* under my bed. Joey got me a subscription. The first issue arrived today. Ma will have a stroke if she sees it.

I wish we'd win ten million dollars. We never have any money. Someday I'm going to be real rich. People think I dress cool, but I could look even better. And I'd buy Ma some stuff. Her clothes are too old. Her boots look like they came from pioneer days. She should get her hair styled and quit perming it herself. It's too long and curly for a person her age.

"I said, are you going out for basketball this year?" She was determined to have a conversation.

"Yeah, but it doesn't start until December. This is October, Ma, remember?"

"I know what month it is, Shepherd. There's no need to be snippy."

Ma's not into sports. She doesn't get the rules, and she always feels sorry for the team that loses. I've told her: Ma, whether you like it or not, life is about competition, winning or losing, that's all it is. Not if you play in a band, she said. I wanted to go out for football but she wouldn't let me. She was afraid I would get hurt.

"I might not go out for basketball this year," I said. "I want to get a job. But I need my license."

"Shepherd, you're not even sixteen yet."

"I will be, soon."

She ignored that. She said, "I want to talk to you about Jack."

"Not now. I'm trying to eat my dinner."

"That's exactly the attitude I mean. Why are you so rude to him?"

"I'm not."

"You never talk to him."

"What's there to talk about?"

My mother's mouth got tight but she kept it shut until the waitress put down our main course and left.

"I won't put up with that attitude," she said. "Lately it's impossible to talk to you. You either make jokes or try to change the subject—"

"No I don't," I said. "Look, there's Elvis!"

"Joking is not conversation," Ma said. I could hear her counselor talking. "Jack and I—well, I like him a lot."

"What's that got to do with me?"

"You're my son. And . . . oh, I don't know. I mean, how would you feel if . . ."

They got married? Like slashing my wrists. Or his. Have a guy in your house you don't even know, telling you what to do all the time? Forget it.

"It's just that Jack and I . . . there's nothing definite . . ."

I tried to listen to what she was saying but I didn't want those words in my mind. I glanced around the restaurant at the other diners. At the far end of the room was that girl from Santa Barbara. Lucia was at a table with her parents and little brother. She had noticed me too. She was smiling.

I think she's so pretty. She's really cool. She's not like the other girls at school. She doesn't wear lots of makeup or jet-puff her bangs. Her hair is shiny and clean and smooth. I'd like to ask her out. We could go to a movie. She could ride there on the back of my bike. Yeah, sure.

Ma's gone and Lucia's at the table with me. We have an elegant restaurant all to ourselves. An orchestra dressed in tuxedos is playing. The tablecloth is white and shines with candles and crystal. A smiling maître d' fills our glasses.

We're gazing so deeply into each other's eyes that I can read Lucia's thoughts. She's thinking: "I love you, Shepherd. You look sensational in your new clothes. I'm so happy that you won the Money Marathon Sweepstakes. Now we can buy your mother a mobile home and park it in the middle of Montana. Then we'll begin a life of our own; you and me, together forever."

Ma said, "I hate to tell you this, but there's an incredibly long hair sticking out of your nose."

"What?"

"Right there."

"Will you get your finger out of my nose?" I felt like everyone in the place was staring at me.

71

"I thought you'd want to know."

"Thanks for the news flash." Lucia could probably see it at her table. *I would've married him, but he had this incredibly long hair* . . . I left for the bathroom, feeling eyes on my back. I put my face close to the mirror and yanked.

"Now it's bleeding," Ma said when I got back to the table.

I can see it, years from now, when Ma is on her deathbed. I'm hunched over, clutching her hand. Her weary old eyes scan my face. She whispers, "Shepherd, you'll always be my baby."

"No, I won't."

She coughs, tries to speak. Her strength is fading. "Son, there's something important I have to tell you."

I can barely hear her. I lean close.

"Promise me you'll always remember this, son. Don't forget to trim the hair in your nose."

She quietly dies. I'm shaking her, frantic. "Ma, don't go! Can you hear me, Ma? There's something I always meant to tell you! Jane called and left a message! Thirty years ago! I forgot to write it down! I thought I'd remember!"

"Jane called last night," I said. "She wants you to call her back."

"Why didn't you write down the message, like I've asked?"

72

"I thought I'd remember."

"You never remember!"

"I'm remembering right now," I said. "She said something about being held for ransom."

That's how it is with me and Ma lately. She jumps on every word I say. Things were better before Jack came along. Now she's worked up about that all the time; does he really like her? Is it going to work out?

Who cares? The guy is not exactly Mr. Excitement. She could find someone better. Or she could be by herself. I hate the way everything's changing.

"Why do you resent me, Shepherd?"

"I don't resent you. Why are you always picking on me lately?"

"That's a laugh!" she said. "It's the other way around. You jump on every word that comes out of my mouth. It's like talking to a lawyer. I know something's bugging you. Why won't you tell me what it is?"

"Nothing's bugging me, except conversations like this." I didn't want Lucia to see us fighting.

"You seem like a stranger," Ma said. Her eyes were shiny. "But I can't stop being your mother now, just because it's hard and I don't know how."

"Just relax," I said. "It's no big deal." Things were getting out of hand. I didn't want her to cry.

"I know you're upset about seeing Joey—"

"He's got nothing to do with this," I said.

"He's been sending you money."

"So what? He's rich. He's just trying to make me like him."

"He needs your love. He wants the whole world to love him."

"Yeah? Well, they never will."

"That's the problem," Ma said. "You have to try to understand him."

"Why? When's he going to try to understand me?"

"Joey's not sensitive to other people's feelings."

"That's the understatement of the century."

"He wants you to go down there and spend the weekend," she said.

"Why, so he can shave my head?"

"What do you mean?"

"Nothing." I'd never told her what had happened to my braid. "Anyway, if he wants me to come down there, he shouldn't ask you, he should ask me. I'm not a baby. I have a life of my own. Maybe I don't want to see him."

If I visit Joey, we'll go out to eat. He never eats at home; his fridge is empty. We'll stay up late. He'll buy me stuff. We'll go to the club. He'll take me to a movie. He's trying hard to be Mr. Groovy.

Part of me wants to slug him. Part of me wants to scream in his face: Where the hell were you all those years? You dumped me like a dog! You couldn't be bothered! Now you want me to say that none of that matters. It matters! A hell of a lot!

The other part of me wants to see Joey; the soft sucker side, the little kid. I like it when I make him laugh. He says I'm funny. You sure take after your old man, he says. That makes me feel so good my chest swells up like a balloon. A big balloon just begging to be popped.

"I thought we could have a nice dinner," Ma said. "I thought we could be happy."

"We did. We are. Here, have a fortune cookie."

"Baby, I—"

"I'm not a baby," I said.

"Can't you tell me what's wrong? Why won't you let me help you?"

"Nothing's wrong," I said. "Anyway, talking doesn't help. It just makes you feel worse about your problems."

"No, it doesn't. That's why I'm going to a counselor."

"That's fine for you," I said. "But I'm not you. I just want things to be normal."

"Whatever that is." Ma sighed. We opened our fortune cookies. Ma's promised love and romance and travel. Mine read: "Be yourself and you'll always know what to do." If only that were true. I smashed and ate the cookie.

You want to talk normal? I'll tell you what's normal. Look at Lucia and her family. They're talking and laughing, not crying and arguing. They'll drive home in a nice car and sleep in the same house. Which won't leak when it rains or be falling apart. Why can't that be us?

On the way out, I turned around and looked at Lucia. She smiled at me and waved her hand. If felt as if she'd tossed me a bouquet of flowers, or the keys to a car that could take me anywhere, that could go five hundred miles per hour.

CHAPTER
NINE

Dear Lucia, also known as Lucy,

I wish I could write to you instead of Mrs. Bloom. This journal business is for the birds. It's a waste of time. I would never write down what I really think. People might use it against me. They say they want to know what you think but if you tell them, they get mad or upset. Or they feel sorry for you. I hate that.

Things aren't so bad for me, compared to other people. I saw this woman on TV; she's been completely paralyzed all her life. They put her in a mental hospital when she was a kid. Her mind was fine but she couldn't talk so people thought she was retarded. Now she's written a book about her experiences, using a fancy computer. She showed her helper each word she wanted by blinking her eyes.

When you see someone like that, you think: boy, I am really lucky. There's nothing wrong with me. Sometimes I even feel like I'm pretty good-looking. Other times I feel like the geek of the week. Too tall, and my legs are kind of skinny. The other day the coach said I run like a giraffe. I don't think he meant it as a compliment.

But some girls seem to like me. Do you like me, Lucia? You were smiling at me at the restaurant tonight. I wish we could've had dinner together. I wish I knew what you were thinking.

Of course, you don't know what I'm thinking either. At school I hardly act like I notice you at all. Too bad you're hanging around with Sheila. She's probably told you I'm a real jerk. I'm just mad because she got my job. My mother won't let me learn to drive. I'll be sixteen next month (are you sixteen yet?) and all my friends are getting their licenses. My mother must think I'm a maniac or something. She treats me like a baby. My father said he'd talk to her about that but he hasn't. He always says he'll do stuff then he forgets.

Do you know who my father is? I hope you don't. You probably don't watch much TV. People think he's a big deal because he's a comedian. But when you see him in person he's not too funny. He's going to have his own TV show soon. He read me part of a script. It was stupid. He's sure it's going to be a big hit. He wants them to call it "The Joey Young Show" but the producers are leaning toward "Beauregard and Me," Beauregard being this obnoxious Irish setter. Joey hates dogs. He thinks they're worse than kids. "They just slobber and crap and beg you for food, and you can't send them away to college," he says. He uses that in one of his monologues.

The other day I was looking at this magazine. Some women were standing in a mountain stream, naked. They weren't doing anything dirty; they were just getting clean. I kept picturing how pretty you'd look, with your long hair wet and gleaming. You'd look like the queen of the forest.

Not that I picture you naked. You're usually wearing clothes. I picture us going to the mall or to the movies, walking around holding hands and stuff. Do you ever have those kinds of thoughts? I wish I had the guts to send this to you, but your dad would probably drive over here and kill me.

Lately I can't concentrate in school. There's too much going on. My mother's always asking me what's wrong and this guy she's seeing keeps coming around. When he's here it doesn't feel like my house. And my dad's back. You'd think I'd be glad, but it's almost worse than when he was gone. Then

I could just say, that's how it is. He was out there, somewhere. I hardly ever thought of him. I missed him a lot when I was a kid. In those days I had all these stupid fantasies that he was going to come home someday, and stay. It was like I kept waiting and waiting. But you know how it is when you don't eat for a long time? At first you're really hungry then the feeling goes away.

Lucia, I feel so weird sometimes, like I'm sad and I can't get happy. I'm always making jokes in class but that isn't the real me. Life seems so crazy. You look around and see all this stuff going on, killings and problems and babies starving, and you're not supposed to let it bug you. You're supposed to say: That's life. I keep wishing God would show up and straighten things out but he's like the Abominable Snowman or something. We know he's out there but we can't find him. Just try to book him on the "Tonight Show."

Maybe what I'm saying doesn't make any sense. I should hit the hay. I'll see you tomorrow. I probably won't even say hi, don't ask me why.

I wish I knew what you were thinking. I'd like to ask you out. But what if you said no? I'd feel so stupid. I might even say, Hey, I wasn't serious, then we'd both end up feeling like fools.

Good night. I hate to say good-bye. I wish I could

talk to you in person. And remember: Don't believe all the bad stuff Sheila says about me. She's been in the pool so long it's waterlogged her brain. Just kidding.

Yours truly,
the great Shepherd Youngman

CHAPTER
TEN

Ma and Jack dropped me off in front of Joey's apartment building. When I got upstairs he grabbed me and hugged me. He was jumping around like a little kid.

"We're on, Sport!" he shouted. "It's in the bag! We sign the contracts next week! The show starts filming in a couple of months! Oh, Shep, I can't tell you what this means to me!"

"That's great, Dad," I said. "Congratulations!" I'd never seen him so happy. Even his eyes were smiling.

He said we were going out to celebrate. We always go out when I visit Joey. The apartment's just the place where he stores his clothes.

I put my things in my room. After a couple of months, it's starting to look more like me. There's some color in the room; a red throw rug on the floor, a bright blue comforter on the bed. Plus a few posters that Joey bought me, and a tape deck so I can play my tapes.

"Where shall we go, Sport? You name the place."

"I need to get Ma a birthday present."

"It's her birthday? Sure, we'll get her something. But where do you want to eat? La Scala? Trader Vic's? Or do you want to see a movie first? There's a Billy Crystal at the Presentation. It's getting killed in the reviews," he added gleefully.

"Maybe we could go to the zoo," I said.

"The zoo? Why do you want to go to the zoo?" Joey quit smiling.

"I've never been there," I said.

"You've never been to the morgue, either. There's nothing at the zoo but a bunch of animals. You want to see animals, we'll go down to the wharf and throw some peanuts at the tourists."

"I'd kind of like to go to the zoo," I said.

"That's kid stuff."

"I'm a kid. You said I could pick."

"You're right. I did. But I didn't think—well, sure, why not. Sure, we'll go to the zoo. That's great. Just let me make a few phone calls first, okay?"

My father loves to talk on the phone. He calls up people just to say hi, like otherwise they might forget he's alive. He called his agent, then a couple of women who'd left messages on his answering machine. He told them his TV show was going to start filming. "Of course I love you, baby," he told each of them, winking at me.

Finally he was ready to go. We took the elevator down to the garage and got the car. Then we had to go by the club. It's closed in the daytime, so no customers were around. He talked to Frank the bartender, then he had to make a few more phone calls.

I was trying to figure out what to buy for my mother. She needs a lot of stuff but everything costs so much. She doesn't like me to spend my money on her. She says, "Just write me a poem or make me a drawing, honey." She used to plaster my drawings all over the fridge, and mailed copies of my stories to her folks back east. We don't get to see her family often. Her folks don't like to fly and Ma can't afford the tickets. They could send her the money, but they don't. They weren't too happy when she married Joey. They're the kind of people who hold a grudge.

"Okay! Let's go!" Joey lit a cigarette, then we got in the car and drove to the zoo. It was a typical November day in San Francisco. The sun hadn't burned through the fog until noon so the air was still moist and cool. The sky was blue and the place was packed with kids; tugging on their parents' hands, pointing and shrieking. Look, there's an elephant! Look, there's a lion! Look, there's an ice-cream man!

I suddenly felt incredibly dumb; like a giant in Tiny Tot Land. I'd wanted to go to the zoo when I was little, and Joey said he'd take me but he didn't. Ma wouldn't; she hates the idea of zoos; wild animals being penned up in cages.

The animals didn't look too happy. The panther paced back and forth. The bears were huddled in a corner. Some kids were throwing popcorn at the monkeys until an attendant came by and told them to knock it off.

Joey was having a wonderful time. Some people recognized him and asked for his autograph. He never turns anyone down. "I can't see these people who won't sign autographs," he says. "They'd be nothing without the public."

He introduced me to some tourists from Indiana, then he posed for pictures with every member of the family. "It's so exciting to meet a real celebrity!" they said. Joey beamed, and when we walked away, he rested his hand on the back of my neck. He's so short it must've been a stretch.

"You know, Shep," he said as we strolled along, "this is how I always thought it would be. You and me. Things are falling into place. It's like—" He stopped walking and lit another cigarette. He looked different than he usually does. Less tense. "—It's like, you work all your life and make sacrifices, and you keep thinking it's going to work out some day. But

85

there's no guarantee. You just keep trying. And then one day, it's like everything clicks. Everything just fits together. I mean, I know you blame me for leaving you when you were a kid—"

"No, I don't," I said.

"Let's be straight, okay? I know you blame me and you should. I was a jerk. Though God knows I used to wish my father would go away. It was like: He's leaving on a business trip! Hooray! We'd celebrate. My mother would fix all this stuff for dinner that she usually wouldn't make, because he didn't like it. He was the king, you know, and we were the peasants. I got tired of that crap. But now it's like I'm my own person, and I can be who I am, and that's damn good. I'm good at what I do, Shep. I know it. Things are finally going my way. So what I'm trying to say is, I know I let you down, but I didn't mean to."

"That's okay," I said. I was scrunched down so his hand wouldn't slide off my neck. Some people who went by recognized Joey. But for once he seemed to notice only me.

"It's not okay," he said. "I should've been there for you. At least I should've been around. Your mother and I—it didn't work out. That's another story. It wasn't her fault. She's a good woman and she did a great job raising you. I knew she would. All she wanted out of life was to be somebody's mom. And I wanted all this other jazz too. But you turned out terrific. I mean it, you're one helluva kid. I'm so proud of you!"

Joey sat down on a bench. I sat down beside him. Kids with balloons swirled all around us. My father's eyes were wet. I touched his leg.

"It's no big deal," I said. "Everything turned out okay."

"Yes, it did." Joey patted my knee and nodded. "Everything turned out fine. I was always afraid you'd end up hating me or something. But the thing is, Sheppy—look at those planes."

Three air force jets were passing overhead, writing lines as white as chalk across the sky.

"The thing is, Shep," my dad continued, "I had to do what I did. There was a voice inside me, saying: You can make it. Make what, you might ask. A fool of myself. I make a fool of myself for a living! Who in their right mind would be a comedian? You fail and you know it right away. The audience is sitting there, just staring at you. Or they're booing, or throwing things. I got hit with an ashtray." Joey touched his forehead, cringing at the memory. "But now everyone is *smiling* at me. It's like everything I touch is music. You know? And I can give you all the stuff— stuff I never had. I can send you to some fancy college. I can send you to the moon, if this show works out! Do you understand what I'm trying to tell you?"

"I guess so." My father's hand was still on my knee. This was different than our usual talks. Usually it's just, did you like the movie, where do you want to eat, things like that.

"No, you don't," he said, " 'cause I'm still waltzing around. Why is it so hard to say? I love you, Shep. You're number one in my book. And I'm just sorry it took me so long to realize how much you mean to me. Can you ever forgive me?"

I had imagined this moment so many times. My father would finally say he loves me, and beg me not to hate him. I would laugh in his face. I would tell him how he'd hurt me, list the endless disappointments, show him pictures of that stupid little boy who just kept waiting and waiting. It's too late, Joey, I had planned to say; I gave up on you a long time ago.

But I hadn't.

I said, I mumbled, "I love you too."

The words hung in the air like a big balloon.

Then we both got busy. We jumped up and moved around. "Okay!" Joey kept saying. "All right!"

We left the zoo and had dinner in a real nice restaurant. The maître d' was pleased to see Joey. He gave us a table where everyone could see us, and brought Joey a telephone. He called the club and talked to the bartender. He said, "Frank, I'm going to be a little late. I'm having dinner with my son."

There was a guy playing the piano. He and Joey were friends. He asked Joey to help him sing a song. Joey's no singer, but the people loved him. When he finished, everyone applauded. So did I.

That night I watched the show from the back of the room. When Joey introduced me, I stood up and took a bow. He said, "Me and my kid had a big fight about money today. He's finally agreed to raise my allowance."

Then Joey did a bit about Halloween. Even though he's thirty-five, he said, he was still short enough to go trick-or-treating. "You remember how we used to go home and count our haul?" he said. "Dump it on the bedroom floor and check out all the goodies? It's different today. You go to the emergency room. The X-ray technician was really impressed! I got three Milky Way bars, six razor blades, two popcorn balls loaded with broken glass, and three packs of mint-flavored Ex-Lax!"

We got back to the apartment late. Joey listened to the messages on the answering machine. Three were from women. He shrugged and grinned at me. "I have a terrible problem," he said. "I'm irresistible."

"Me too," I said. "It runs in the family."

While I brushed my teeth, he hung around in the doorway, smoking a cigarette and sipping a drink.

"Shep," he said finally, "I want to ask you something. You don't need to give me your answer now. Just think about it. That's all I'm asking."

I was expecting a punch line. But Joey said, "I want you to come and live with me. If you want to. It's up to you."

I stood there, with my mouth full of toothpaste. I didn't know what to say. Then I remembered that I hadn't gotten my mother a birthday present.

CHAPTER ELEVEN

My mother's birthday is a week before mine. She didn't seem to mind turning thirty-seven. Jane and Jack came over for her birthday celebration. Jane brought lasagna, salad, and French bread. Jack brought two bottles of champagne. They toasted each other and joked about Ma's age while I sipped ginger ale.

I hadn't told Ma about Joey's invitation. There hadn't been a way to work it into the conversation. Oh, by the way, Ma, I'm moving to San Francisco. She'd probably grab my legs and refuse to let me go.

If I wanted to go. What did I want to do? I racked my brain every day. Someone would feel bad, no matter what I decided. I wished that Joey had never come back. I wished that he had never gone away.

I couldn't concentrate in class. I was driving Mr. Munson crazy. One day he'd been going on and on about how TV had totally wrecked teenagers, how they expected life to be constant entertainment.

He said, "The trouble with you cheeseheads is that you have no attention span. Thanks to the blab box, your brains are attuned to twelve-minute segments of sex, violence, and car crashes. Wouldn't you say that's true, Youngman?"

"Sorry," I said. "I wasn't listening."

Everyone laughed, except Mr. Munson, who looked like he was going to spontaneously combust.

"You're a real comedian, aren't you?" he snarled.

"Like father, like son," I said.

I ended up in the vice principal's office. Mr. Miller sighed and shook his head.

"You've got to quit mouthing off in class," he said. "What's the matter with you this year?"

"I wasn't mouthing off. I just wasn't listening. When I told him, he had a fit. I'm not going to sit there without saying something back."

"That's important if you're on a talk show," Mr. Miller said, "but it's not appropriate in class. It makes you look like a wise guy." He gave me another detention.

I am definitely not feeling like a wise guy lately. I don't know what to do. If I live with Joey, it will break

Ma's heart. If I don't, I know it will hurt his feelings and I'll probably never hear from him again. How could I leave Ma? But Joey was finally showing some interest. I'd waited a long time to have a father.

I tried to talk to Swampy about it. He didn't understand. "You'll probably get to be on his TV show," he said. "I bet he'll even buy you a car. Geez, I'd love to get out of Santa Rosa!"

True, Santa Rosa wasn't too exciting, but Ma had her job there and I had my friends. I kept remembering all the stuff Joey had said at the zoo. I'd wanted to say a lot of stuff to him, but I was afraid I would start crying.

I'd have to talk to Ma soon. But not tonight. Happy birthday, Ma. By the way, I'm leaving.

"Shepherd, you're awfully quiet," Jane said. Her eyes were sparkling with champagne.

"He's probably thinking about his girlfriend," Jack said.

"I don't have a girlfriend."

My mother smiled. "Jack means that young lady you're always talking to on the phone."

She meant Lucia. "I hardly ever talk to her," I said. "I was just asking about our assignment."

"Every night?" she said.

"It's not every night." I was not in the mood to be teased.

"Methinks he doth protest too much," Jack said.

"Methinks I don't care what you thinks," I told him.

"Shepherd!" Ma said.

"I was just joking."

She looked like she didn't believe me. But she didn't want to hassle, she wanted to party. She was full of dinner and cake and champagne, with a pile of packages to open, including a box of stationery from me. Ma likes to use nice note cards.

There was a bathrobe from Jane and a pair of earrings. Jack gave her a plant and some books and tapes. Ma acted like each gift was just what she'd been needing. She raved about the stationery so much that I wondered if it was ugly. Look what my kid gave me. Isn't it funny? Did you see his drawing on the fridge?

I couldn't get into the party mood. I felt like I was letting her down. We'd always been close. Now my father was between us. Why did Joey want me to live with him? Couldn't he just get a budgie? Or maybe a machine that would laugh and applaud whenever he pushed a button?

After Jane and Jack left, Ma came into my room. I was at my desk, pretending to study.

"Such a nice time," she said, sitting on my bed.

"Yeah."

"What're you doing, honey?"

"Some reading for science."

J. Robert Oppenheimer directed the team that developed the first atomic bomb. He didn't want it used; it was supposed to be a deterrent. The government wanted to drop the bomb and kill people, not just scare them to death. No one knew for sure what would happen when the bomb exploded. Some scientists believed it could ignite a chain reaction which would blow up the whole world.

The government went ahead and made the bombs and dropped them. So we blew up the world? So sue us.

"Shepherd," Ma said, picking at my bedspread, "I need to talk to you about something."

I hate it when she says that. I never know what's coming. It could be anything from, I'm dying of cancer, to, Son, your deodorant isn't working.

"Honey, I've been thinking." Ma brushed something off my shirt. "You're getting to be a pretty big boy—"

"Wow, do you think so?"

"Almost sixteen years old. I swear, I can't believe that. One second, you were a little baby, and now, before you know it, you'll be going off to college— Shepherd, will you look at me, please?"

"I'm listening." I was having trouble meeting her eyes. I was afraid she would see Joey in mine.

"What I'm trying to say is, you'll always be my baby, but—"

"Ma, I'm not a baby."

"Will you listen to me? That's the point I'm trying to make, if you'll just shut up. You can take driver's training. It's okay with me. I'll sign the permission slip. Are you surprised?"

I was stunned. "Did Joey talk you into this?"

"No. I haven't heard from Joey in weeks. I've been thinking about it, and I talked to Jack and Jane. You're a responsible young man. What's the matter? Aren't you pleased?"

"Well, yeah, but I can't take driver's training now. It's booked up till next semester."

"You can start then," she said. "In the meantime, Jack said he'd be glad to take you out in the car. You'd probably be too nervous with me. You can go way out in the sticks and practice shifting and parking. And you can study the manual. See?" She put it on my desk. "I picked it up at the DMV. I was going to give it to you on your birthday, but I couldn't wait. You know me and secrets."

"That's great, Ma. That's really good. But the thing is—it's too hot in here." My turtleneck was choking me. Our house is usually freezing. Ma leaned toward me, snuggled in her new robe, smiling so wide I could see her teeth. Her folks should've gotten her braces. "The thing is, I might not be here next semester."

"Where would you be? Are you planning to run away?"

"Not exactly," I said. "Don't get mad, okay? But Joey wants me to live with him, in San Francisco."

Her smile faded. "I don't understand."

"It's not like I'd be very far away. I'd come home every weekend, and on the holidays, and I'd be here in the summer ..."

Ma's face had suddenly aged. She looked seventy, not thirty-seven.

"Joey's talked to you about this? He's got it all arranged?"

"He asked me last weekend. I was afraid to tell you."

My mother's eyes were huge and full of questions. She hugged the robe around her. She looked down at her bare feet.

"Do you want to live with Joey?" she almost whispered. "Is that what you want?"

"Yes and no. I want to stay with you too. But he's different now, Ma, and he told me some stuff. Like how I'm important and he loves me. He really said that. It wasn't just an act."

"Your father's always loved you," my mother said,

rocking back and forth as if her stomach hurt. "He's always cared about you, Shepherd. I've tried to let you know that. He just wasn't cut out to be a full-time dad."

"But now that I'm big, it doesn't matter," I said. "It's not like he needs to hold my hand. And I'd be going to a really good school. It's a school of the performing arts, so I could learn to play the piano. He said he'd get me one. If I move down there, I mean."

I've wanted to play the piano since I was a kid, but we could never afford it. Ma always said she'd get me a baby grand when we won the Money Marathon Sweepstakes.

My mother stood up. Then she sat down again. She said, "I don't know what to say. You're a big boy, Shepherd; old enough to make your own decision. I just thought—"

"Don't be sad, Ma. I won't go."

She shook her head no and shut her eyes.

"I'm sorry," she said. "I don't mean to cry. I'm just surprised, you know? I wasn't expecting this."

"Me neither. It's just that Joey—well, you know how he is. I wasn't going to tell you on your birthday. It just slipped out."

"Surprises have a way of doing that. I had to know sometime." Ma tried to smile.

"I haven't told him I'll go. I said I'd think about it."

"You have a right to know your father." My mother sighed. "You missed him so much when you were a little boy. You'd ask me why he didn't come see you or call. Sometimes I didn't know what to say. It wasn't that he didn't love you. It was just that what Joey wanted always came first. Now he's older, maybe wiser. Stranger things have happened. This was inevitable, I guess."

"I won't go if you don't want me to," I said.

"No, that has to be up to you. I'm not into guilt trips," Ma said. "If I didn't do what my parents wanted, they made me feel like a bad person. It worked like a charm but I always resented it. I'm not going to do that to you, baby."

"I'm not a baby." I was trying to make her smile.

"You'll always be my baby, no matter how old you get. Even when I'm an old lady. Even when I'm dead. Oh, Shepherd, I'm sorry. Champagne makes me weepy." She brushed away the tears as if they made her angry.

"Anyway," I said, "it wouldn't happen right away. I don't want to start a new school in the middle of the semester. Joey says I'm real smart and that it wouldn't matter. He wants me to move over Christmas vacation."

"Good old Joey. He's got it all worked out," Ma

said. "It would've been nice if he'd discussed this with me first, but I've never been a top priority with your father."

"He thinks you're a good woman. He told me."

"Well, that's a relief." My mother laughed and kissed the top of my head. "Don't worry, bunny. It will work out fine."

"I don't want you to feel bad."

"Oh, I'll be all right. I love you, honey, and I know you love me. That's what's important, and it's never going to change. You better get some rest. We'll talk more tomorrow. And thank you again for my beautiful stationery. It's so pretty I'll want to keep it for myself."

She kissed me again and moved toward the door. Then she turned around and said, "There's something you need to understand, Shepherd. If you move to the city, you'll have to give it a fair chance. You can't move there one day and come back the next. Of course you'd be a little homesick at first, but later on you might like it. We'll see. If you don't, you can come home when the semester is over. You'll always have a place here, honey. I won't be renting out your room."

I said, "Dad would feel bad if I decided not to stay."

"Joey's a big boy. He can take care of himself. He

wants you to be happy, and so do I. You have to do what's right for you."

"Ma, you've been talking to your counselor again."

"Good thing," she said, closing the door. "Sleep tight, bun."

For a long time, I kept sitting at my desk, trying to focus on my science book. It didn't make sense. I knew how Oppenheimer must've felt. Why did Joey wait so long to love me?

C H A P T E R
T W E L V E

For my birthday my father gave me a truck. He pulled into the driveway that Sunday afternoon in this nice clean '85 red Nissan pickup. He honked the horn a bunch of times. My mother and I went to the door to see who was outside.

"Happy birthday!" he shouted, tossing me the keys, which almost hit my mother. She went back into the house.

"What do you think, Sport? Don't you just love it?" My father was still shouting, even though I was standing beside him. I ran my hands over the hood.

"Is this for me?"

"No, I traded in the Galaxie. Of course it's for you! Do you like it?"

"Well, yeah!" I couldn't believe my eyes. I couldn't stop smiling. "There's only one problem—I don't know how to drive."

"No problem!" Joey was grinning. "You're getting your learner's permit, right?"

"Yes, but not until I take driver's training."

"We'll just take it out for a spin," my father said. "Get in."

"But Ma—see, I'm having some friends over tonight."

"We're going for a ride, not cross country. We'll be back in a couple of hours. Run inside and tell your mother so she won't worry."

I'd never been behind a steering wheel in my life. Don't worry, Ma. No problem. Really.

"Well, see, her boyfriend said he'd take me out sometime."

"You'd rather learn to drive with him?" Joey frowned.

"No, but we haven't—"

"I thought you'd be pleased. I mean, I knock myself out—"

"I'm pleased! It's just that—"

"Tell your mother we'll be back by five."

She was standing at the kitchen sink, doing dishes. Even her back looked mad.

"Dad wants to take me out to show me how

103

the truck works. We'll be back by five. Is that all right?"

"You don't have your permit."

"I won't go on any roads. We'll be back in plenty of time. The guys won't be here till six." They were coming over for pizza and movies.

She still hadn't looked at me. "What about your homework?"

"I've done it."

"Then do what you want."

"It's a real nice truck," I said. "You can use it to go to the dump."

My mother turned around. Her face looked tired.

"It's a beautiful truck. I know you love it," she said. "But he should've checked with me first, before he went out and bought it."

"It wasn't my idea."

"I know that, honey. It's just that . . . what's the use. I give up." She went back to doing the dishes.

"I'll be careful." I went over and kissed her cheek.

"Bye, honey. Have a good time," she said.

My father drove us out into the country. He stopped in an empty parking lot beside a church, where there was plenty of room to drive around. Then we traded places. I had to move back the seat; my knees were practically under my nose.

"Go ahead." Joey lit a cigarette. "It's easy."

104

"I've never done this before."

"Your mother's never let you steer?"

"No."

"Geez, talk about a deprived childhood! I could drive by the time I was thirteen," Joey said. "I snuck out with the car once. I thought my dad was asleep. I come back—he's standing in the garage with this look on his face—I thought he was going to eat me! Anyway, it's simple. There's the clutch, there's the brake."

"Where?"

"Right there." He sounded faintly annoyed. "Okay, turn the key. Not like that. Now put your foot on the gas. The gas, not the brake! Oh great, you've stalled it."

"Dad, will you lighten up? It's the first time I've tried!"

"I thought you'd at least know how to start a car."

"Just give me a chance!"

"Don't shout at me, Shepherd."

"Well, don't blow smoke in my face! I can't breathe."

"Is this better?" Joey hung out the window, puffing. "Maybe I could ride on the hood. You could read my lips through the windshield. Would that be good?"

"You're acting like a jerk."

"I'm acting like a jerk? I bought you this truck, now I'm a jerk? I hate to say this, Shepherd, but that really hurts my feelings."

"You're not the only one who has feelings," I said. "I've got feelings too. You treat me like an idiot, no matter what I do."

"That's not true!"

"What about that basketball game at the park?"

"What about it? I was trying to be helpful! All I said was—"

"I know what you said!" We were steaming up the windows.

"All I said was that everybody who wants to play basketball doesn't get to be Dr. J. Am I right?"

"Just like everybody who wants to be a comedian doesn't get to be Bob Hope."

"Who wants to be Hope? He's yesterday's news! What're you trying to tell me?"

"Look," I said, "I want to learn to drive, but it won't work if you keep yelling. Just relax and give me a chance, okay?"

"Okay," Joey said. "How's your mother taking it?"

"The truck, you mean?"

"No, the arms agreement with the Soviets. I mean how's she taking the move to San Francisco?"

"She's not too thrilled."

"But you're going to," he said. "Right?"

"I'm thinking about it."

As far as he was concerned, it was all settled. "This tape deck's pretty good," he said. "The speakers are practically new."

"That's good."

This wasn't how I'd pictured my sixteenth birthday. You think that when you're big you won't have any problems. The problems just get bigger and more complicated. Too big for Band-Aids with stars on them.

"Okay," Joey said, "let's take it real slow. You put the key in the ignition. You turn it on."

Slowly and carefully, I drove around the parking lot. It was the most thrilling thing I'd ever done. I forgot that Joey was sitting beside me. I could feel life opening up before me like a shining road.

"There!" Joey announced. "You see? It's easy!"

Nothing's easy, I could've told him.

When my father brought me home, Ma stayed out of sight. She was in the bathroom, taking a shower. Joey came inside to use the telephone. A beautiful woman in a yellow MG came by to pick him up.

"I'll talk to you next week!" he called from the car. "Happy birthday!"

"Thanks for the truck, Dad. But you better park it in the street."

He was speaking to the woman and didn't hear

me. He'd left the pickup behind my mother's car. She'd have to move it when she wanted to get out.

My friends arrived: Swampy, Mike, Rusty, and Ryan. We had clam dip and potato chips and pizza. They each gave me ten bucks. Ma said that was too much but it wasn't.

She gave me some slippers and a tape and a shirt.

"Pretty small potatoes next to a truck," she said smiling.

"No," I said. "That's great. That's fine."

We watched the movies I'd picked out at the video store, where we'd rented the VCR. I could tell Ma wasn't pleased by my selection. Whooom—the ice-cream box hit the counter. Wham—she slammed down the cake plate.

"Shepherd?" she called. "Can I see you for a minute?"

"Sure." I tried to sound real cheerful so my friends wouldn't know there was a problem.

When I got into the kitchen my mother hissed: "You know how I feel about that movie!" We were watching Eddie Murphy in *Beverly Hills Cop*.

"What's wrong with it?"

"It's so violent! And I hate his attitude toward women."

"It's just a movie."

"That's not the point. Every time I look up, I see a naked woman!"

108

"Could you please keep your voice down?"

"It's like those awful magazines. No wonder you're hiding them under your bed. I know who gave them to you, so you don't have to tell me. You realize, don't you Shepherd, that those women aren't normal. Every woman in those pictures is an exhibitionist."

"Ma, can we talk about this later?" I pleaded. If my friends heard us, I was dead.

"There's nothing to discuss. Women are not inflatable sex objects, no matter what your father thinks. Here, take the cake."

My friends hadn't heard us. I could tell; their chins weren't quivering. We watched the rest of the film. Then we talked to some girls on the phone. I didn't call Lucia; she's a secret I'm keeping. When you like somebody a lot, you get kidded. That's how it is.

After my friends left, I helped my mother clean up. Then I sat in the truck, listening to the radio.

The house glowed in the dark like a birthday cake with all the candles blazing. She'd tried to make us sing. Everybody laughed, embarrassed. So she sang by herself. "Happy birthday, dear Shepherd . . ." From the truck, I could see her moving through the rooms. I felt far away, as if she were someone in a movie, an old movie I was watching in one of those big theatres my dad takes me to in San Francisco.

CHAPTER THIRTEEN

Later, I could not remember ever having said: Yes, I'll move to San Francisco. It sneaked up on me, like a change in the weather, like the fog rolling in, gray and cool.

My friends sounded envious and said they'd miss me. It was kind of like attending my own funeral. They said school wouldn't be the same without me. But hey, life goes on! Are you going to Ryan's party? ... Not that I expected my basketball shirt to be flown at half-mast. It was just kind of weird hearing my friends make plans that wouldn't include me.

Mrs. Bloom asked me to write letters to the class, describing my new life in the city. I told her I wasn't much of a letter writer. Ma makes me write thank-you notes for gifts, and once I wrote a letter to Joey but I didn't know where to send it.

I still have it, in one of my bureau drawers. It says,

Dear Dad,
How are you? I am fine. Well, not much is new. I was wondering when could I see you? I heard your record album. It's funny. Well, not much is new, so I'll ~~sing~~ sign off for now.

Love, Your Son,
Shepherd Youngman

In case he'd forgotten who I was.

I didn't tell Mr. Munson I'd be leaving. I was afraid he'd keel over with joy on the spot. I've been trying to stay out of his hair. But even when I'm being nice, he thinks I'm making fun of him.

Sheila's the same way. Since she's friends with Lucia I've been trying to be cool. Not that I act like we're best pals, but at least I haven't stuffed her in a locker.

It's been tempting. In Living Skills the other day, our discussion group topic was "children of divorce." They were discussing it; I kept my mouth shut. No way was I going to be the celebrity cripple.

Sheila turned to me and said: "Your parents are divorced, right? You haven't said a thing."

Swampy and Lucia and the other kids stared at me. My face was burning, but I stayed in control. I said, "I don't have anything to say."

111

"That's a switch. You hardly ever shut up. You go around all the time like the big comedian—"

"My dad's the comedian, not me," I said. "You don't have to worry about your folks getting divorced. Neither one of them would want to be stuck with you."

Lucia looked worried. Swampy looked away. Sheila said, "I guess that's supposed to be funny. Remind me to laugh."

"Just look in the mirror," I said.

Things were going downhill fast. Lucia changed the subject.

I feel bad when I think about leaving Lucia. We went to the winter dance together. Her long green dress was as soft as moss. We danced real close and I could smell her hair.

Ma says: "I can't get a word out of you, but you talk to her on the phone for hours! You just saw her at school! What can you have to say?"

There's never enough time for everything we have to say. Lucia has a great sense of humor. Sometimes we laugh for no reason; just because we feel so good.

We stopped by Gartini's the other day, after school, and Mrs. G. said, "You guys are so cute!" When Lucia wasn't looking Mrs. G. winked at me and did something that looked like the hula.

I'm going to miss Lucy so much when I move. We'll talk on the phone and I'll be home every weekend, but it won't be like seeing each other every day. She'll probably find somebody else.

Joey's the only person who's really excited about the move. He can't wait for it to happen. I feel like his latest fad. He gets superenthusiastic about something for a while; a trendy new restaurant or a hot band, then he loses interest, they're old hat.

He took me to Tahoe last weekend. We were supposed to ski but the snow was lousy so we ended up in the casinos.

I can't gamble, of course, but he did, for hours. I was too young to even be there but they didn't kick me out. Joey's a celebrity; he's played all the big rooms. The rules don't apply when you're a star.

Waitresses in teeny little outfits kept bringing him free drinks. "This is my kid," he'd say, jerking his thumb at me when he wasn't throwing dice or pulling levers.

"How old are you, Shepherd?" the waitresses would ask, batting their false eyelashes.

"Not old enough for you!" Joey would say to uproarious laughter. As they walked away, their butts twitching, he'd nudge me in the ribs and say, "You like that? Pretty cute."

My mother would've had a fit if she'd seen me. "Number one," she would've said, "you're too young to be in a casino. Number two, they're temples of greed. Number three, you shouldn't be looking at women in their underwear."

As far as she knew, we were only going to ski. I never go into all the details.

We got in an argument on the way home. I said I wanted to go to Disneyland sometime. Joey said he'd already taken me.

"No you didn't," I said.

"What're you talking about? You shook Mickey Mouse's hand!" Joey was indignant.

"You never took me to Disneyland. I'd remember something like that."

"Obviously not." He punched the cigarette lighter as if he wished it were my nose. "This is the thing that burns my butt. I take you someplace, we have a great time, and then you say you forgot!"

"How old was I?"

"Who are you, Perry Mason? How should I know? Maybe three or four."

"I've never been to Disneyland," I insisted.

"Are you calling me a liar?" Joey's face was getting red.

"If you took me, how come there aren't any pictures?"

"I didn't have a camera, okay? If I'd known you were going to require proof, I would've hired a film crew! Don't you remember, we went on that mountain thing, what do you call it, and Mr. Toad's Wild Ride—"

Joey raved on. I tried to remember. Ma would've mentioned it, unless she hadn't known. There are lots of things that Joey doesn't tell her.

I'd wanted to go to Disneyland forever. Ma said we would, when we had the money, but we never had the money when we had the time. On vacations we went to the beach or camping. Gram and Grampa took me to see Hearst Castle. I'd pictured me and Ma living in those elegant rooms, swimming in that cool, silent pool.

Mom, I used to say, I'll be real rich someday and I'll buy you all the stuff in the world. We'll have a plane and a train, and you won't have to work. Don't worry, I'll take care of you.

Joey was babbling about riding in a tram and going to Tomorrow Land. For some reason, I was thinking about this time with my mother, when we'd bought the Perfect Loaf of Bread.

We were on our way to Goodwill to get me some clothes, so it must've been a while ago, before I realized that wasn't the trendiest place to shop. We stopped at a bakery and bought two loaves of French bread; one for now and one for later.

The bread had just been baked. It was soft and warm and fragrant. It was the best stuff we'd ever

115

Cynthia D. Grant

tasted. "The food of the gods!" Ma said, rolling her eyes. She called it the Perfect Loaf of Bread.

"Oh, honey, it doesn't get any better than this," she said. She didn't just mean the bread. "I love you so much."

"I love you too, Mom," I said.

How old was I then, nine or ten? We like to remind each other of that day. Sometimes I can almost taste it.

CHAPTER
FOURTEEN

The Christmas tree my mother brought home was the size of a potted plant.

"Where are you going to put it? In the budgie's cage?" I asked.

"There's nothing wrong with this tree," Ma said.

An old lady could've worn it on her coat.

"That's not a tree, it's a branch," I said. "There won't be room for all the ornaments."

She gave me a look. "I went to three different lots. The trees were too expensive. Everything costs so much these days." She went into the kitchen and started supper. "After we eat, we'll string some popcorn for the tree."

"That ought to take about five kernels." The TV was on so she didn't hear me. As usual, all the news was bad. Homeless families, kids without Christmas presents, kids without moms and dads.

117

"Supper's ready," Ma called.

She'd made grilled cheese sandwiches.

"I thought you were going to use cheddar," I said.

"We don't have any, so I used Monterey Jack."

"I only like cheddar."

"Since when?"

"Since practically my whole life."

"That's not true."

"Why would I lie about grilled cheese sandwiches? This stuff really makes me gag."

"My, you're in a lovely mood," Ma said.

"There's nothing wrong with my mood. I'm just pointing out a fact."

"If you don't like what I make, then you ought to start cooking. Can't you turn off the TV while we're eating?"

It was still blabbing in the background. I said, "I want to catch the sports."

We finished our supper. Another show came on; one of those sappy holiday specials, about a family that has fallen apart and then gets back together on Christmas Eve.

"This is so stupid," I said.

"Then turn it off." She was out in the kitchen, making popcorn.

"Something else is coming on in a while," I said. I was trying to get comfortable in the big square chair, hanging out the side so it wouldn't stab me. I felt

118

really beat. There was one more week of school until Christmas vacation. When I left school next Friday, I wouldn't be back. I'd be moving to San Francisco. Ma had wanted me to wait until the end of the semester, but Joey said that wasn't necessary.

"He's a smart kid. They'll average in his grades. He'll do fine," Joey told her. Ma's mouth was a thin line. He'd turned to me, smiling. "What's the matter, Sport? Cold feet?"

I was moving. There was no turning back.

"Shepherd," Ma said, "could you get the box of ornaments? It's in the hall closet."

"Just a minute. I love this commercial. Look at that car! Don't you love that car, Ma?"

"It's okay."

"Okay? Do you know how much it costs? Fifty thousand bucks!"

My mother got the ornaments and then started wrestling the tree into the stand.

"Why don't you put it in a vase?" I said. It was skinny and skimpy and pathetic.

"This tree looks thirsty, hon," Ma said. "You'd better give it a drink."

When I was a kid I thought everything had feelings. I practically went nuts if the tree ran out of water. It made me real sad to see the trees that no one bought lying in the lots on Christmas Day.

"In a minute," I said. The TV show was so stupid

119

I couldn't stop watching it. The old father and his grown sons were having a big argument and the mother was saying, "Please, stop it!" Everyone was acting like something tragic was happening, but you could tell there would be a happy ending. They'd all be sitting at the dinner table together, or around the Christmas tree, singing carols.

"Shepherd, is there something wrong with you tonight?" My mother's eyes were glittering. Not a good sign.

"No, not really."

"Then why are you acting like such a jerk?"

"I'm not acting like a jerk. I'm tired. I had a lousy day at school."

"Gee, that's too bad. I was lying around the house all day, roasting chestnuts and reading magazines. I worked my butt off! Then I went Christmas shopping. It took me half an hour to park at the mall. Then I drove all over the place for a Christmas tree, so I could come home and have you tell me it's crummy."

"I didn't say it was crummy. I said it was small."

"Do you know how much this tree cost? Thirty dollars! It took me three hours to earn that tree! You don't seem to realize that we don't have much money."

"How could I forget?" I said. "That's all you ever talk about."

"Really? Gosh, I hope I'm not boring you. Let's talk about something else instead. Look at me when I'm talking to you. I'm sick and tired of you acting like a slob. I come home, you haven't even done one thing! All you do is mess the place up! I'm sick of finding your fingernails all over the house!"

She was pointing at a tiny pile of clippings on the coffee table as if it were a dead body.

"Those aren't fingernails, those are toenails," I said.

My mother looked as if I'd taken the clippers and stabbed her in the heart.

"I don't care what they are! Either put them in the wastebasket or leave them on your feet! Don't leave them sitting around in piles! Do you hear me?"

"Of course I hear you. They can hear you downtown! Why don't you make a federal case out of it?"

Cut to the courtroom. Ma's on trial for my murder. She sits beside her lawyer, sobbing. On the wall behind the judge, there's a big picture of me. I look incredibly handsome and solemn.

The district attorney approaches the bench. "Your Honor," he says, "I'd like to enter these fingernail clippings as evidence."

"Objection!" Ma's attorney leaps up. "Those are toenail clipppings, your Honor. He'd leave them all over the house. Disgusting! I would've killed him myself!"

The D.A. asks: "What difference does it make what kind of clippings they are?"

Ma's lawyer says, "Plenty! Toes are grosser than fingers!"

"Your Honor, that's strictly a matter of opinion!"

"Oh, really?" Ma's lawyer peels off his shoes and socks. "Well, how would you like to shake my foot?"

"Listen to me when I'm talking to you!" My mother was blocking my view of the TV.

"I was listening to you!" I repeated what she'd said. "I'm just tired of you getting on my case all the time!"

"The feeling is mutual! You're always criticizing me! Nothing is good enough for you. I know you're upset about moving to the city, but that's no reason to take it out on me!"

"I'm not upset about moving! Will you read my lips? Why don't you listen to what I'm saying?"

"Because you won't say how you feel. You keep everything inside," Ma said. "So I have to guess what you're thinking."

"Well, you're guessing wrong." The show was really getting drippy. The kids had just found a lost and lame baby deer.

"My counselor says people—"

"I don't care what she says! That's got nothing to do with me!"

122

My mother grabbed my hair and pulled it hard, her face so close to mine I could hear her breathing.

"Do you want me to hit you? Is that what you want?"

"Yeah, Ma. Sure." Tears stung my eyes. She was hurting me.

"I will not tolerate this kind of rudeness, Shepherd. It is absolutely unacceptable. I love you more than anything in the world, and I want to help you. But I can't if you won't let me."

She let go of my hair. She said, "I'm sorry I grabbed you. But you make me so mad! I have feelings too!"

"Don't worry," I said. "I'll be gone soon. I'm moving."

"Whether you're moving or not, you've got to treat me right, the way that I treat you. I'm not your personal punching bag, Shepherd. I don't take my problems out on you. My counselor says it's normal for people to argue at times like this, so they won't feel bad when they have to separate."

"I don't feel bad," I said.

"Then why are you acting this way?"

"I'm not acting any way."

"It's Christmastime," Ma said.

"What difference does that make? I'm not a little kid anymore."

"I feel like I don't know you." My mother was crying.

"That's right! You don't know me! I'm a big boy

now!" I jumped up. She was so short. "I've changed! Look at this place! It's falling apart! Why do we have to live here? Look at this chair! It's a total wreck! Why can't we get a new one?"

"We don't have the money."

"That's not true! You work all the time, like you're always telling me!"

"I pay the rent! I buy your clothes and food!"

"Well, use some of the money Dad gives you! What are you doing with it? Saving it for college? Maybe I don't want to go to college, did you ever think of that? Maybe I just want to be a bum!"

My mother was shrinking. She got smaller and smaller.

"Your father doesn't give me any money," she said.

"Yes he does! He gives you child support!"

"Your father doesn't give me a dime. The first year we were apart, he gave me five hundred bucks. That's all he ever gave me. That's nothing!"

I said, "I thought he sent you money."

"I was trying to protect you. I didn't want you to know the truth," Ma said. "Joey didn't want kids. I was the one who did, so he said you were my responsibility. If I'd gone after him legally, you would've found out. I was afraid he'd get mad and take it out on you; disappear for good or refuse to see you. I shouldn't have lied to you, honey, but I didn't want you to be hurt. So I kept waiting for your father to grow up. A real smart move on my part, wasn't it?"

Ma turned around and left the room.

I sat down in the chair. My head was spinning. You'd think it would've crossed my mind. Why had I believed that Joey supported me? He wouldn't even call me, most of the time. He's never been rich, but he's always had bucks; enough for fancy cars and boots and restaurants. Meanwhile, Ma's buying her clothes at yard sales, so she can get me the hundred-dollar basketball shoes, the genuine Levi jacket. She got that for me last Valentine's Day. I said, "Thanks, but it's not the style I wanted."

I was furious at Joey. But I was madder at myself. What a stupid little geek, what a chump. Joey disappears for years then flies in on his magic carpet, and what do I do? I eat it up. Oh Dad, it's so great to have you back. Oh gee, do you really want me? You can cut off my hair. You can cut off my mother. Just don't cut me off, Dad. I need you so badly.

The TV mother said, "This is the happiest time of the year!"

The little lost deer wasn't lame anymore. The family took him outside, where his mother was waiting. A big star was shining overhead. The family started singing "Silent Night."

I turned off the TV and gave the tree some water.

Then I put on the Christmas album that my mother really likes; no shrieking sopranos, no Carbuncle Boys Choir, just the old carols, played on a guitar.

I went down the hall and tapped on Ma's bedroom door.

"Mom, can you come out here for a minute?"

"What is it, Shepherd?" Her voice sounded weak.

"It's time to do the tree."

Please. We'd eat all the popcorn and forget to string it. We'd put on the lights and the decorations; the fragile glass balls that belonged to Ma's Gram; the ornaments we'd collected and the ones I'd made in grade school: tattered candy canes and chains of colored paper.

Ma opened the door. Her eyes were red. "Okay," she said, "but you have to put on the lights."

"Oh, man! No way! They're so tangled up!"

"You'll figure it out. You're a big boy, Shepherd, just like you're always telling me."

She padded down the hall in her fuzzy slippers, humming "Joy to the World."

She always gets me.

CHAPTER FIFTEEN

I planned to murder my father when I saw him; to tell him the move was out. He could cry all he wanted; it wouldn't break my heart. He'd left me and Ma behind a long time ago. I was going to finish what he'd started.

Ma said no, I had to forgive and forget. Everybody makes mistakes, she said; maybe he's really changed.

I doubted it. But that day at the zoo kept replaying in my head. When Joey said he loved me, he meant it. He wanted me with him. I'd have to go to a new school. I've seen what happens to kids who transfer in; they're checked out, mostly ignored, occasionally befriended. Joey was the only person I'd know in San Francisco and I hardly knew him at all.

I finished the last week of school in a daze. I didn't know if I was coming or going. The coach said the basketball team would be hurting without me.

"Maybe I'll be back," I told him. "Who knows?"

On Friday I decided to tell Mr. Munson I was leaving, not that I expected him to care. I just wanted to say: Thanks for not killing me. The news would probably brighten up his holiday season.

After class I went up to his desk. He glanced up and nailed me with the oddest smile.

"If it isn't the great comedian!" he said. "Have I got a Christmas present for you!"

I said, "I just want to tell you—"

"I want to thank you, Youngman. You've helped me make a big decision. I'm leaving."

Weren't those my lines? My mouth was hanging open. Mr. Munson crossed his arms and grinned.

"I won't be back after the holidays. Doctor's orders. He says this place is killing me. So I'm taking early retirement, thanks to you."

"Mr. Munson—"

"Just listen." He aimed his finger at my face. "That's the trouble with you kids, you're all mouth. You think you've got the answers. I've got news for you: The world's going to chew you up and spit you out. I've been here thirty years. Things have really changed. Kids today—you're cannibals. Well, you're not getting me. I'm out of here. Merry Christmas, happy New Year, bon voyage."

He stood up, still grinning, locked his briefcase and

left. I felt awful, not that it was all my fault. Over the years, Mr. Munson had had to deal with one cheesehead too many, and it turned out that cheesehead was me.

After school I met Lucia. She tried to cheer me up. We agreed to get together before I left for the city; maybe go out to dinner or to a movie. She said she would drive. I would never learn to drive. My truck sat in the driveway like a practical joke; the world's largest portable radio.

For the next few days I tried to get Joey on the phone, leaving messages on his machine. He didn't call back. For Christmas he sent me a hundred bucks and a card that said, "See you on the 27th, Sport!" He had tickets for a big rock concert that night. He didn't say anything about picking me up so I figured I'd have to take the bus.

My mother and I spent Christmas Day as we have for years, with Jane. Jack came over too. He gave Ma a ring. Not a diamond, thank God, so it doesn't mean anything. He gave me a Knicks hat I'd wanted.

In the afternoon we called Ma's folks and had the traditional conversation: Merry Christmas, Grandma! How's the weather there? Et cetera. I could have the same kind of in-depth discussion with people picked at random from the phone book.

The day after Christmas, we drove to Sacramento.

Cynthia D. Grant

Ma's always gotten along with Joey's folks. When she told them I was going to be living with Joey, my grandfather looked like his dinner was coming back up.

"Carolyn, do you think that's wise?" he asked.

"Shepherd has a right to know his father," Ma said.

"His father gave up any rights he had, long ago!"

"Joe, please, we're having a nice time," Grandma said. Needless to say, they hadn't heard from Joey.

When we got home I phoned Lucia. Her mother said she was visiting her cousins. I tried Joey again and got the same old message: "Hi! I'm too important to come to the phone right now, so at the sound of the beep, leave your name and a credit card number and I'll get back at you as soon as possible!"

"Dad, it's me," I said to the machine. "I'll be down there tomorrow, in the afternoon. Call me if that won't work out."

I started packing some of my stuff. Ma came in and helped me. We're getting along extremely well. Too well. I would've given anything if she'd acted normal; screamed at me about my room ("You call this a room? It's a pigsty! A pig would complain to the Humane Society!"), or had started a fight. Instead she was incredibly polite, as if she wanted everything to be perfect, so she could remember me that way.

My father never called back so I assumed we were on. Ma drove me to the bus station and dropped me

130

off. I watched her drive away in her clunky little junker, waving and wearing this frozen smile like the one on her driver's license.

I ignored the crazy guy seated beside me on the bus, who kept brushing lint or invisible ants off his clothes, and tried to figure out what I would say to my father.

Why didn't you give Ma any child support?

I didn't have any money, he'd say.

In fifteen years you never had any money? What do they give you for being on TV, room and board?

I wasn't on the tube that much.

You were playing clubs. You were making records and movies!

Who are you? The I.R.S.? I was barely making ends meet!

That's a lie. Look at Ma. Look at the car she's driving! You're telling me you had less money than she did?

You're welcome, Shepherd.

Welcome for what?

For your Christmas money. And the damn truck. And all the other stuff I bought you!

I'm not talking about now! I'm talking about then! You couldn't send her something, even fifty bucks a month? One time we were so broke she sold her blood!

I couldn't win, but I'd have to try. At least he could

131

reimburse her. She could buy a decent car and some new clothes. Maybe she could take a real vacation, go to Hawaii or on a cruise or something. Joey could afford it. He'd be making big bucks on the TV show. He'd make more in one week than she did in a year.

I took a cab to Joey's apartment building. He didn't answer when I knocked. I let myself in with the keys he'd given me. The curtains were drawn and the place was dark. It looked like the cleaning woman hadn't been there recently. The coffee table was overflowing with dirty dishes, ashtrays, and Chinese food cartons.

"Dad?"

There was an empty bottle of Scotch by the couch. I was getting scared. "Dad?" I called again. I heard the toilet flush. My father came out of the bathroom. His clothes were messed up, his hair was greasy. It looked like he hadn't shaved for a week.

"Shepherd." He looked puzzled. What're you doing here?"

"It's Wednesday, remember? We're going to the concert. What's the matter with you? Are you sick?"

"Sick to death," he said. "Sick of everything. Care to join me in a glass of champagne? Don't worry; it's a big glass, we'll fit. That's a joke, son. Get it? No, he just don't get it."

He waded past me, into the kitchen. There was an open bottle of champagne on the counter. He looked around for a clean glass, but everything was dirty so he rinsed out a coffee mug and filled it.

"Bottoms up," Joey said. "Happy New Year."

"Dad, what's the problem? Why are you drunk?"

"If only I were drunk. But I'm not, that's the problem." He shook his head and finished his drink.

"What's wrong? What happened? Did somebody die?"

"Nobody important. Just me. They killed the damn show." His voice was thick with disappointment.

"What do you mean, they killed it? You signed the contract!"

"It's dead, I said! Didn't you hear me? Do I have to spell it out? D-E-A-D. I'm history, I'm finished. Do you know what they did?" Joey was so mad he was reeling. "They decided to go with a kid-and-doggy show! They wanted me to be the nutty neighbor who pops in to tell a joke! I told them: It's my show or I'm out! And you know what they said? This is some world! You lose everything! You don't even get to keep your teeth! Look at this hairline!" He bared his forehead. "It's disappearing faster than the rain forests! You want topical humor? Or is that tropical? I'm telling you, I'm losing it, I'm washed up. Once the news gets around about the show, it's all over. Nobody wants a has-been. I think I'm going to be sick."

I thought he would make a run for the bathroom,

but he staggered into the living room and collapsed on the couch, covering his face with his arms.

I sat down next to him. "What's your agent say?"

"My agent? That traitor! He sold me out! Told me we had to play ball with the network! I said: I'm taking my balls and going home!"

"It's not the end of the world." I was trying to cheer him up.

"It's not?" Joey snarled, sitting up and glaring at me. "Then it's doing a first-class impression!"

"You still have the club."

Joey waved the words away.

"I thought you liked the club."

"It's like the airport," he said. "It's okay to hang around there for a while but eventually you want to take off. I mean, what am I supposed to do now? Be the doorman at Caesar's Palace? 'Hello, folks, you probably don't remember me. I'm the official celebrity has-been.' Or maybe I could be a game show panelist. That's where comedians go to die."

He looked terrible. I didn't know what to say. He rubbed his face hard and said, "I need a drink."

"You don't need a drink. You need something to eat."

"Hey, who's the father here, me or you? I say I want a drink, I want a drink. Where's my smokes?" He pawed through the mess on the coffee table then reached under the couch and grabbed a pack. It was empty.

"All gone. The story of my life," he said. "Go down to the corner and get me a pack. Where's my wallet? Do you have any money?"

"Yes, but Dad—"

"Don't sit there and argue! Just do it!"

"But Dad—"

My father's face crumpled. "Oh, Sheppy, I had it all! Now I've got nothing!"

He was sobbing. I'd never seen him cry, I mean really cry, as if his heart had cracked and everything inside it was spilling out. I patted his back.

"Don't worry, Dad," I said. "You'll get another show. You'll be fine. That other show was stupid. Don't worry, Dad."

After a while he sat up and put his arms around me. The top of his head barely reached my chin.

"Sheppy, you're all I've got," he said. "You're the only thing that matters. I mean it. The business is so phony. It's all a big act. You think people like you then they knife you in the back, but hey, don't take it personally. Who needs it? I don't need this kind of grief. You're the only person I can count on, Sheppy. You're the only thing I need."

"You still want me to live here?"

"No," Joey said. "I want you to come in once a

week and clean. Of course I want you to live here! That's the plan, isn't it? You and me, we're a team. We'll have the best comedy club in the world. You'll see. They'll be lining up around the block to get in. Who needs that stupid show? The scripts were terrible. That god-awful dog. And now they're bringing in a kid! Play second banana to some little brat? And my agent's telling me I'd better settle for a walk-on. I told that jackass—"

"Dad, you need a bath. No offense."

"Yeah, just a minute. I've got to make a phone call. I'm going to tell that jerk—make me a sandwich, will you, Shep? There might be something in the fridge. Or, here—" He dug a ten-dollar bill out of his pocket. "Go down to the corner and get us some groceries. Whatever you want. Some eggs and bread. And a quart of milk. My stomach's killing me. And get me a pack of Kools, okay?"

Joey was smiling as he dialed the phone. "It's just like you said, Sport. There are big things ahead. They haven't seen the last of old Joey Young."

He winked and gave me the thumbs up sign. Then his agent answered and Joey started yelling.

CHAPTER SIXTEEN

My mother loves Jack and the feeling is mutual. They hug and smile all the time. They're going to get married someday. I know it. Once I'm out of the picture, Jack will ooze in the door. It's a good thing I'm moving to San Francisco. The last thing I need is a stepfather.

Jack took me out in the truck so I could practice my driving. We went way out in the sticks, on a country road where there were hardly any cars. Unlike the time when I was driving with my father, Jack remained completely calm.

"You're doing fine, Shep. Take it nice and slow," he said, humming. That humming gets on your nerves after a while.

I was blowing it, stuttering from one gear into the next. Joey would've flipped if he'd been there. It's a truck! he would've shouted. Not a pogo stick!

"Let's take a break," Jack said. "Park right up there."

I steered the truck over onto the shoulder of the road and almost into a drainage ditch. Jack leaned out his window and sniffed the air as if it was full of flowers.

"So, are you ready for the move?" he asked casually. They're taking me to the city tomorrow.

"Not quite. I haven't finished packing," I said.

He nodded as if I'd answered his question. I knew what he'd meant; he was asking how I felt. As if there was a chance that I'd tell him.

"You're doing fine with the truck."

"Yeah, right," I said.

"Will you be able to take driver's training at your new school?"

"I guess so." I couldn't picture learning to drive in all that traffic, or shifting into first on those impossible hills. The truck would slip out of gear; I'd plunge down the hill backward.

"Your mother and I are really going to miss you. But I hope it works out for you," Jack said.

"I'll bet."

"What's that supposed to mean?" He screwed up his face. He's not good-looking and that expression didn't help.

"Nothing."

138

"No, tell me. I want to know."

"You probably can't wait till I'm gone," I said.

Jack looked surprised and a little mad. "Turn off the engine so we can talk," he said.

"There's nothing to talk about."

"Turn it off."

I did. It got so quiet in the truck I could almost hear his hairline receding. It's worse than my dad's.

He said, "I'm sorry you feel so bad lately, but don't take it out on me. I want to hear anything you've got to say, but I'm not your whipping boy. Got me?"

"Yes."

"Don't you want to move, Shepherd?"

"Sure. I guess."

"You're not sure?"

"I guess I'm sure! What difference does it make what I think? It's happening."

"Not if you don't want it to. It's your decision. What do you want to do?"

"I don't know," I said.

"If you don't like it there, you can always come back."

"Not until the end of the semester."

"That's because your mom wants you to give it a chance. Otherwise, you'd always wonder if it could've worked out. I know you resent me, but—"

"I don't resent you."

"I'm not competing with you, Shepherd. I'm not pushing you out. You're Carolyn's son," Jack said. "She loves you so much. And I love her, and I'd like to be close to you, if you'd let me."

"I've already got a father."

"I'm not trying to be your dad."

"Neither is he." Sometimes I feel like Joey's big brother.

"I'm never going to take his place," Jack said. "But maybe someday I'll be your stepfather. If you decide to move home again, we'll work things out. Life doesn't have to be so black and white, Shepherd. We can all have a good time together."

"I doubt it."

"Suit yourself," he said. "Don't you want to be happy?"

"What I want doesn't really matter!" My voice was rising. I was losing control. "You and Ma don't need me around! And Joey—it's like I'm his stunt-man or something! I'm the one who gets hurt, not him!"

"Is that what you think?"

"I don't know what I think."

"You don't have to move. You can change your mind."

"And have my father hate me forever?"

140

"Your dad wouldn't hate you."

Maybe not, but he'd say that I'd let him down. If I decided not to move, there would be no second chance. It was now or never with my father.

"It's fine," I said. End of conversation. "We'd better get back to town."

We stopped by Gartini's so I could say good-bye. Mrs. Gartini hugged me so tightly I thought my nose was going to bleed.

She said, "I'll miss you, kiddo! You come back and see me."

"I'll probably be home every weekend," I said.

"Once you get your license you could do the Saturday deliveries. Sheila's thinking of quitting."

Swell. Just when things are falling into place, I'm leaving.

We got home. Ma asked, "How did the driving go?"

Jack said, "He's doing really well."

I said, "I stink."

"Did you see Darlene?" Ma was trying to smooth my hair. "She wanted to ask you about delivering."

"Yeah, I know." I moved away from her. "But I might not be home every weekend. I guess I better finish packing."

"Lucia called again."

I didn't call her back. I hadn't gotten around to seeing her. What was the point? Everything was ending.

I went into my room and locked the door and turned on the radio. Music pounded out, hard and loud. They didn't ask me to turn it down. I turned up the volume until the room filled with sound and there was hardly enough room left for me.

CHAPTER
SEVENTEEN

My mother and Jack moved me and my stuff to San Francisco. Joey wasn't at the apartment; he'd left a note saying he had to go to the club. The real reason, of course, was that he was avoiding my mother, in case she was having a nervous breakdown or wanted to punch him in the nose.

It took several trips to carry my stuff up to the apartment. Then suddenly the job was done.

"I guess that's it," Ma said. Jack went down to take another look in the truck. For once, I wished he'd stuck around. I didn't want a big scene with my mother.

I showed her all the rooms.

"Too much," she said. "We're talking megabucks."

"It's close to school," I said. "I can walk or take the bus."

"Did Joey get you registered and everything?"

"Oh sure. He said he'd take care of it."

"Well, I guess that's it," she said again. "I'll be seeing you, bunny."

"I'm not a bunny."

"Will you give me a break? You'll always be my bunny." She had her arms around my neck like she was drowning.

"Ma, this isn't goodbye forever. I'm not going to the moon. I'll be home next weekend."

"I know," she said. "It's just that—you're a big boy now, aren't you, Shepherd."

"Don't worry," I said. "I'll be fine."

"I know. I'd better go." She started backing toward the door. "Call me this week and let me know how it's going. Honey—"

"Don't worry!"

"I'll see you." She was gone. From the window I watched the truck pull out of the garage and melt into the traffic. Then I squared away my room, filling the closet and bureau drawers. That took a couple of hours. Then I called the club. Joey wasn't there. I was hungry but there wasn't much to eat. I ate cheese and crackers and some fancy nuts, washed down with a bottle of tonic water.

Joey came home around five o'clock. He headed straight for the answering machine.

"Sport, how's it going? It's great to see you!"

He seemed to have recovered from losing the

show. His hair was freshly styled and he was wearing new clothes. I hadn't told my mother that the show had fallen through. Joey likes people to think that things are super-duper.

"I put away all my stuff," I said.

"Great. We'll go out and get some chow in a minute." He finished playing back his messages. "All set. Are you hungry?"

"Starved." My stomach was growling.

"I did an interview today, with a guy from the *Chronicle*. He's a jerk, but he writes okay. It should turn out pretty good. Where do you want to eat?"

"Any place they've got food," I said.

"Maybe we better get some groceries tonight. I swear, this kid's got a hollow leg. If I ate like you, I'd weigh five hundred pounds. Why don't you write up a list while I make a phone call? We'll get out of here in a minute."

I'd never made a grocery list before. My mother does all the shopping. I tried to remember what I like to eat. When Joey saw the list, he groaned and said, "I'll have to stop by the bank and take out a loan."

We walked to a restaurant a few blocks away. The night was cold but so full of neon lights that it wasn't really dark. The sky was pink.

The sidewalks were crowded with people, some going places, some just hanging around. A wino was passed out almost in the street. Joey told me to not make eye contact with weirdos, and that if people started begging, I should ignore them.

"What if they're hungry?"

"The whole world's hungry. What're you going to do, invite it home for lunch? You give these guys money, they'll spend it on booze."

We passed a woman standing in a doorway. A little girl was sitting at her feet. The woman held a sign that read: PLEASE HELP ME FEED MY BABIES. But we didn't stop, we just kept walking.

The restaurant was cozy and full of well-dressed people. We got a good table and Joey ordered a drink. For dinner I had spaghetti and he had prime rib. There was enough food on our plates to feed that little girl in the doorway for a week.

I wanted to ask him about the child support but I wasn't ready to start fighting. I'd say this and he'd say that, and in the long run, it wouldn't make any difference. He couldn't change the past. Maybe Ma was right, and I had to forgive and forget. Forgive, anyway. I would always remember.

"Are you excited about starting school tomorrow?" he asked.

"Not really." Smoke was blowing in my face. He keeps a cigarette going while he eats.

"What kind of attitude is that? You'll never get ahead that way."

"I won't know any of those people."

146

"So? It's better that way. They've got nothing on you. You can start from scratch."

My stomach was tight. I wasn't hungry anymore. "Did you talk to the people at school?"

"About what?"

"You said you were going to register me."

"I figured you could do that when you went." Joey lit another cigarette.

"You said you'd do it!"

"I've been busy, do you mind?"

"You told me you would!"

"So sue me!" Joey said. "I hate to tell you this, Shepherd, but you're not the only guy on the planet. I've been taking care of a few little things. Like earning a living, for instance. Who do you think's paying for all that food? The food you're not eating, I might add?"

"You couldn't make a phone call? You make a hundred a day!" The people at the next table were staring at us.

Joey leaned close. His smooth pink cheeks were gleaming. "Would you get a grip on yourself?" he hissed. "You go in there tomorrow, you sign up. No big deal. Does Daddy need to hold your hand?"

"No, but you said—"

"I know what I said!" Joey threw himself back in his chair, exasperated. He started talking loud, playing to the crowd. "Something came up! I've been working on a deal. If this thing comes through, you can forget

147

about school. You can drop out and start spending money, full-time. My own prime-time show, Sport. No kiddy co-star. No dog. The dog is out. Incredible scripts. The best writers in the business. We're this close to making a deal. And I've been busy with the club. What do you want me to do? You knew how it would be when you moved here, Shep. Anyway, you're not a baby, you're fifteen."

"Sixteen."

"That's my point exactly. You're a big boy now. Will you lighten up? Things are going to be fine. I mean it! I know you're nervous about going to the new school, but wait till those kids get a look at you. You'll knock them out! I know what I'm talking about. Trust me!"

I should've known Joey wouldn't do what he'd promised. I had known, deep inside. He's like a magician. It's all an illusion. Enjoy the act but don't look too close. Watch the Amazing Joey pull another TV show out of his hat! Now watch him saw me in half. I'm bleeding.

He said, "I thought you liked spaghetti."

"I guess I'm not hungry." It was lying on my plate like a pile of orange worms.

"Well, you'll have to finish it if you want some dessert. This place makes terrific cheesecake. Listen to me!" Joey laughed and shook his head. "I sound just like a father."

148

CHAPTER EIGHTEEN

Joey wasn't up when I left for school. I didn't know which bus to take so I walked. The wind was fierce and made my eyes water. I wore the Levi jacket Ma gave me, wishing I had something warmer.

I saw some other kids heading toward the school. Their eyes slid over me. They didn't wave or say hi. Neither did I, I kept my hands in my pockets.

The school was huge and ugly. I walked up the stone steps and down a long hallway lined with lockers. I didn't know where to go. There were kids all around me, laughing and talking, but I didn't want to ask them for directions.

A woman told me the main office was down the hall. I walked into the room I thought she'd meant. It wasn't an office; it was a class, in session. The teacher stopped talking. Everybody turned around and stared at me.

I must've looked shocked, because a few people laughed. "Sorry," I said, and made a quick exit. The class laughed again. The halls were almost empty. A man came by and frowned at me. "You're late," he said, tapping his watch. "Get going."

Something weird was happening: I was having trouble breathing. My heart was hammering and my face felt hot. I walked out of the building and down the stone steps. Turn back, I thought; you're going the wrong way. But I just kept walking faster.

It was freezing on the street. The air was thick with fog. A lot of people seemed to be camped on the sidewalks. They were wrapped in ragged coats and blankets. A woman in a short dress came up to me and said, "Ten bucks. Whatever you want, ten bucks." A bunch of old guys spare-changed me.

I kept walking and walking. My nose was running. I had to wipe it on my sleeve. My mother's always telling me to carry Kleenex. My mother. My mother. I almost called her. I stood in a phone booth, holding the receiver, until a guy came by and tapped on the glass. I thought he needed to use the phone but he was making a pass.

Maybe I was sick. My forehead was burning. I had to get back to the apartment and lie down. Where was the apartment? Maybe miles away. When Joey left for work I could go back and get in bed, and pull the blankets over my head. What was happening to me?

I went into a deli and drank strong coffee, and read the newspaper from front to back. I bought a roast beef sandwich and ate it. A cop came in and I got real tense, as if he knew that I was cutting school and was there to arrest me. Then it hit me: nobody cared what I did. Nobody knew me; I was just another stranger. I could drop out of school. I could fall through the cracks and no one would put out a hand to stop me. I could wander through the streets with tears on my face. Nobody was going to ask me what was wrong. They were only going to ask me for money.

I was back on the street. I felt terrible, crazy. I was acting like the nuts I was supposed to avoid. You are such an idiot. You are such a baby, I thought. I tried to make myself go back to the school but my feet wouldn't take me.

I got on a city bus. The driver was arguing with a passenger. I ducked out of the way so I wouldn't get punched. The driver was huge. He threw the passenger off. The guy ran along beside my window, screaming. We left him in a belch of exhaust.

I got off at the ocean, the end of the line. I'd gone

151

as far as I could go. The sea was gray and rough. The beach was deserted. My pockets were empty. I'd have to walk home, meaning back to Joey's apartment, wherever it was. I felt as if I were a million miles from Santa Rosa.

I went into the zoo. The wind was freezing. The snack shacks were closed. There were no kids around. I stood behind a fence and watched a lion watch me. He looked so sad I started crying.

I'm sorry, I told him, I'm really sorry. I'll never come to the zoo again. If it wasn't for idiots like me, he'd be free, running across a golden plain. We should've left him alone. We destroyed his home. He doesn't belong in the city. He's dying.

CHAPTER
NINETEEN

I didn't call my mother that week. What could I tell her? Great news, Ma: I've dropped out of school! She would've known something was wrong as soon as she'd heard my voice.

Joey asked me no questions and I told him no lies.

"How's it going, Sport?"

"Okay."

"That's terrific."

This went on all week. I hardly ever saw him. He got home from the club after I was asleep and was still in bed when I left in the morning.

I'd walk a few blocks to a cafe called Mom's. The owner, Mohammed, made a great Spanish omelet. While I ate my breakfast, I'd read the *Chronicle*.

Then I'd go to the library or to a museum or the movies.

I never went back to the school.

At first, I felt like a fugitive; my heart in my throat, my palms sweaty. My life was over. I was a high school drop-out. I felt like a statistic in the newspaper articles about the bleak future of American youth.

By Friday, the situation didn't seem so tragic. It seemed stupid. Here I was, playing the Troubled Teen, like some refugee from reality, while my father, played by Joey, was completely unaware (nothing new there) of what was going on. It was the kind of situation that would make Ma laugh if she saw it in a movie. In real life, starring me, she'd miss the humor.

This could've gone on for years. Joey wouldn't have had a clue.

How's it going, Sport?

Terrific, Dad.

By the way, did you ever finish high school?

Sure thing, Dad; a few years ago. Then I went to college and attended law school. Now I'm a famous attorney.

I'd seen less of Joey since I'd lived with him than I had when I was still with Ma and he was making guest appearances. He's won my love. But it's not enough. He wants the world. The other night he said, "No matter how funny you are, there's always one guy in the crowd who's not laughing." That's the guy he's after; the heckler, the holdout, the eternal stone face. My grampa.

I knew my father loved me. What more did I want? A lot more, maybe, but I wasn't going to get it. When I was little, Joey promised to buy me a toy plane. You could sit in it and pedal and pretend to fly. I wanted it so much. He forgot all about it. Why did I still want it? What good would it do me now?

Joey will never be father of the year. He'll always be Joey. I'm the one who's changed. I had to pull myself together. But how?

I walked the city streets and looked at the people. On Monday, everyone had looked desperate and sad. By Friday, I could see that they were smiling. Nothing terrible was happening to me. I was going through some changes, that was all. Sure, the city was different from Santa Rosa, but it wasn't the Twilight Zone. It was full of interesting people, and things to do and see. I wasn't giving it a chance. I was acting like a baby. It was as if I'd gone into a fabulous restaurant and insisted on ordering bread and water.

Friday afternoon I went to the movies and saw a couple of old comedies. I laughed until I was weak. I came out of the theatre feeling light and clean. The afternoon was bright and sunny.

I walked back to the apartment, figuring out what I had to do. On Monday I'd go back to school. I wouldn't get in trouble for cutting; they hadn't been expecting me. The last week was a lost week but it wasn't a disaster. I'd concentrate on my studies. I'd learn to play the piano. Eventually I'd make some friends.

When I got home I'd call Ma and tell her everything was fine. I'd even ask how Jack was, and say that I hoped they'd get married. It wasn't fair for her to be alone. And if Jack made her happy, for some unknown reason, that was fine with me. I pictured the conversation and how pleased she would be. I'd skip over the part where I'd skipped school.

Maybe I'd even tell Joey the truth. That would be a novelty. He'd make a lot of noise about me cutting class but he wouldn't really care.

He was on the phone with his agent when I got to the apartment. For a change, he wasn't yelling; he was laughing. Not his fake talk-show chuckle, but the real thing.

"Oh, Sheppy!" he shouted, hanging up. "This is it! Wait till I tell you! This is unbelievable! I've got a show! Friday nights! No kids, no dogs! The Joey Young Show! Starring you know who! What a way to start the new year! Can you believe it? We're going to celebrate tonight, I mean it!"

"That's great, Dad! That's fantastic!" I was glad to see him happy. He's waited for this moment all his life. He looked ten years younger. He looked younger than me. Everything was finally going right.

"You'll have to tell your mother. We'll be moving next week. She won't be too thrilled."

I said, "Moving where?"

He lit a cigarette. "L.A."

"Los Angeles?" I sounded like he'd punched me in the throat.

"No, Lower Albania. Of course I mean Los Angeles. That's where we're shooting the show."

"Why can't you do it here?"

"Nobody makes shows here. L.A.'s where it's happening. You know that."

"But what about Mom?"

He looked horrified. "You want me to ask her to move down there?"

"I mean, how can I see her if we move to L.A.?"

"The same way you'll see her now, on the weekends. You can fly up a couple of times a month. You're going to love it there, Sport!"

"I thought you hated Los Angeles."

"No." He laughed. "Just the people."

I said, "I don't understand."

"What's to understand?"

"I thought you wanted me to live with you!"

"I do! What's the problem?"

"You didn't even ask me if I wanted to move!"

"We don't have any choice! What's the matter with you?" Joey waved his arms in the air. "This is the chance of a lifetime!"

"Yeah, for you," I said. "What about me? I'll never get to see Ma. It'll kill her if I move so far away."

"Sheppy, what can I say? Life is full of tough choices."

"Not for you."

"What's that supposed to mean?"

"You only care about yourself! You probably forgot all about me till I walked through the door! Then it's like: Oh, there's Shepherd. He'll have to come with me. Or maybe I could put him in a kennel—"

"Will you quit acting like a baby?" Joey ground out his cigarette. "I thought you'd be happy for me. I thought you'd be pleased."

"You didn't think of me at all!"

I was breathless, panting. I wanted to hit Joey. I wanted to smash his famous baby face into the floor.

The phone rang.

"Don't answer it," I said.

"Are you nuts? What's the matter with you? It might be important."

"The answering machine's on. You can call them back."

"I hate to say this, Shepherd, but I'm very disappointed."

"You're disappointed?" I was screaming. "What about me?"

He backed toward the phone. He said, "You're acting crazy."

A man's voice came out of the machine. "It's me again, Joe. Pick it up."

"It's my agent." Joey reached for the phone.

"I don't care who it is! Call him back! We're not done!"

"Shepherd, you don't understand," Joey said. "I need this show. I want this show. I want it more than anything I've ever wanted in my life."

"Yeah, including me."

But he was talking to his agent. "Ted?" he said. "Yeah, I'm here. Hold on a sec . . . Shep, I'll be with you as soon as I'm through. We'll talk some more. We'll go out to eat. You pick the place. Things will be fine, you'll see. I'm telling you, you're going to love L.A. Seriously."

I left the apartment while he was still on the phone. He didn't see me leave. He never sees me. When the spotlight's in your eyes, it makes you blind. *That's the funny part, Shep; you can't really see them. But you know they're there, 'cause you can feel them smiling. For a while they forget about their awful lives. The world's a terrible place, let's not kid ourselves, Sheppy. So when you make them laugh— I'm telling you, you feel like God.*

I took a cab to the Greyhound station. I had to wait quite a while for a bus headed north. The place was jammed with nuts, but nobody bothered me. Laugh and the world laughs with you. Cry and you'll get to sit alone.

It was late when I got to Santa Rosa. I walked home along the dark familiar streets. I found the hidden key and let myself into the house. Ma had fallen asleep in bed, reading.

I touched her shoulder gently. I didn't want to scare her. WOMAN DIES OF HEART ATTACK; SPOILS HAPPY REUNION.

"Ma, it's me."

Her eyes rolled open. "Honey, what are you doing here? Did your father bring you?"

"Kind of. It's late. We'll talk tomorrow. I just wanted to let you know I'm home."

"How's school going? Why didn't you call me?"

"I dropped out of school. I went to the movies all week."

160

"Very funny," she said. "You sound just like your father."

"Don't say that."

"Honey, what's the matter? What's wrong?"

"Nothing." I was sick of bawling like a baby. I wanted to laugh. It was all a big joke. Joey was just a banana peel and I fell for him every time. "Oh, Mom," I cried, "he's leaving me again."

CHAPTER
TWENTY

I was sitting on the couch, watching my father's TV show. It was warm outside and the sky was still light. My mother and Jack were supposedly washing her car. Instead, they were squirting each other with the hose, running around like a couple of nuts. You'd think they were ten years old.

The phone rang as Joey was coming in the door. The real phone, I mean, not the one on TV.

It was Lucia. She was wondering if I wanted to get something to eat.

"Sure. I'm watching my dad's show. Have you seen it yet?"

She said, "Last week."

"How'd you like it?" While I spoke, Joey was standing on his head.

Lucia hesitated, but she's truthful. "The jokes were

pretty bad," she said. "Especially the one about him starting a kennel to raise guard dogs and guide dogs."

"And he ends up with a mixed breed that attacks blind people? I thought that was kind of funny," I said.

"You did? Well, a blind person wouldn't."

"A blind person wouldn't be watching TV."

"Now you sound just like the show," she said. "You asked for my opinion."

"It's the number five show in the whole country." Joey called me up the other night and told me that himself.

"You must be proud of him," Lucia said.

"Who wouldn't be?" At that moment he was dropping his pants.

Sheppy, things are going so great! he'd said. I wish you could be here with me. I went to this party the other night—you know who was there? You wouldn't believe it! You should've seen the food! You would've gone crazy. Why don't you come down for a visit?

I've got a job, Dad. I'm delivering groceries.

Just for a week or two, that's all I'm asking. I promise I won't kidnap you and sell you into slavery.

I told Mrs. Gartini I could work all summer.

Talk about slavery! Then come for the weekend. Come for lunch!

Maybe, I told him. We'll see.

Lucia said, "Come by after the show."

"I can leave now," I told her. "I know how it turns out."

I picked up my truck keys. The studio audience roared with laughter. A big dog was licking Joey's bug-eyed face. I left the show on; I can't turn off my father. He's part of me, he's in my blood. He'll always be back, like a cold sore, or Christmas. *Hey, that's pretty good, Sport; do you mind if I use it?*

On the TV Joey said, "See you later, Alligator!"

"In a while, Crocodile," I said, and walked out.